BO AT
BALLARD CREEK

KIRKPATRICK HILL

ILLUSTRATIONS BY LEUYEN PHAM

SQUARE
FISH

HENRY HOLT AND COMPANY

NEW YORK

*I'm indebted
to Arnold Captain for his bear story—
Arnie was the one who fell down flat
and his dad, Billy Captain, did the shooting—
to Harold Tilleson for checking all the mining facts,
and to Alan James, wireless expert.*

**SQUARE
FISH**

An Imprint of Macmillan
175 Fifth Avenue
New York, NY 10010
mackids.com

Square Fish and the Square Fish logo are trademarks of Macmillan and
are used by Henry Holt and Company under license from Macmillan.

Square Fish books may be purchased for business or promotional use. For information on bulk
purchases, please contact the Macmillan Corporate and Premium Sales Department at
(800) 221-7945 x5442 or by e-mail at specialmarkets@macmillan.com.

Library of Congress Cataloging-in-Publication Data
Hill, Kirkpatrick.
Bo at Ballard Creek / Kirkpatrick Hill ; illustrated by LeUyen Pham.—First edition.
pages   cm
Summary: "It's the 1920s, and Bo was headed for an Alaska orphanage when she won the
hearts of two tough gold miners who set out to raise her, enthusiastically helped
by all the kind people of the nearby Eskimo village"—Provided by publisher.
ISBN 978-1-250-04425-9 (paperback) / ISBN 978-0-8050-9894-5 (e-book)
1. Alaska—History—1867–1959—Juvenile fiction. [1. Alaska—History—1867–1959—
Fiction. 2. Fathers—Fiction. 3. Adoption—Fiction. 4. Eskimos—Fiction.]
I. Pham, LeUyen, illustrator. II. Title.
PZ7.H55285Bo 2013 [Fic]—dc23   2012046055

Originally published in the United States by Henry Holt and Company
First Square Fish Edition: 2014
Book designed by April Ward
Square Fish logo designed by Filomena Tuosto

1 3 5 7 9 10 8 6 4 2

AR: 5.2 / LEXILE: 840L

In remembrance of Clarence Zaiser,
a gold miner for sixty years,
and for my family, who've all, at
one time or another, gone mining:
Matt, Kirk, Mike, Suzanne, Sean,
Kiki, Shannon, and Steve

—K. H.

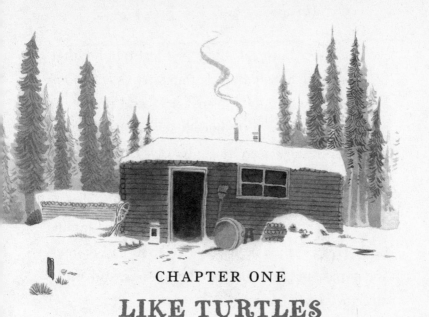

CHAPTER ONE

LIKE TURTLES

BO HAD TWO FATHERS and no mothers, and after she got the fathers, she got a brother too. But not in the usual way.

HER TWO FATHERS were Jack Jackson and Arvid Ivorsen. They'd come to Alaska with the 1897 Klondike gold rush when they were young, a long time before they got Bo. The girl Jack was going to marry had died, and Arvid had just buried his mother, so they didn't have any reason to stay where they were.

They were both extra big. Not just tall, not that beanpole tall, but that kind of massive tall, six four or six five, with huge, deep voices and powerful, big fists. And they were both blacksmiths, her two fathers. But those were the only ways they were the same.

Of course Bo figured out when she wasn't too old that her family was not like any other family in Ballard Creek. The Eskimo children had mamas and papas, and grandmas and grandpas, and aunts and uncles and cousins.

"Do I have a mama?" she asked one day.

"Well, everyone has a mama," said Jack. "But sometimes mamas don't stick around, you know. Just walk off. Lots of animals like that." He was quiet for a minute, trying to think of an animal that took off, didn't hang around. "Turtles," he said suddenly. "Where I come from, they got big turtles, lay their eggs in a hole, just walk away."

Bo considered that. "Did my mama walk away?"

"Sure did," said Jack, "and lucky for us, someone giving away babies. Just what me and Arvid needed."

Bo knew about giving away babies. Gracie had

given her baby girl, Evalina, to Big Jim and Dishoo, because they didn't have any babies and Gracie had two and one was enough.

So that was enough of an answer for Bo when she was little.

JACK HAD A REAL NAME: Gideon. But when he came up north, he right away got the name Black Jack—because he was black, and a blacksmith besides, and his last name was Jackson. He liked that name fine because he didn't like the name Gideon. Arvid was called Swede by nearly everyone, or Big Swede, because he was.

Everyone had nicknames in those Klondike days. It was very popular. Jack used to tell Bo some of the crazy names and how people got them, to make her laugh. Like Tin Kettle George and Slobbery Tom and Pete the Pig and Calamity Bill. The dance-hall girls all had nicknames too, Jack said, like Gold-Tooth Gertie and

Rompin' Rosie. Jack said nicknames were good for the girls' business.

Bo called Jack Papa and she called Arvid Papa. No one remembered how she'd decided on Papa, but it was right about the time she learned to talk. She was too little to understand that nobody would know who she was talking to if they were *both* called the same thing, so that's the way it stayed. Papa for both of them. And actually, somehow it didn't get mixed up at all.

Jack and Arvid knew each other first because of the shirts.

After he got to the Circle Mines, Arvid got himself a sewing machine. His mama had taught him to sew, and he was good at it. He figured he could make good money sewing shirts for the men in his off time from blacksmithing. And he did. The dance-hall girls even got him to sew this and that for them, though Arvid said they were much fussier than the men.

When Jack came to work at the Circle diggings, he heard about the shirt maker. Right away, he looked for Arvid to sew him shirts because Jack was a big, big man. His arms were as big around as some women's waists, and his neck was as big as some men's legs. So he couldn't just buy shirts from the trading post.

When he found Arvid sewing in a room in the back of the saloon, they both started to laugh because they didn't very often see a man as big as themselves. Arvid, in fact, found he could make Jack's shirts to the same measure as his own. Jack was happy that Arvid knew that big men needed some extra reinforcement at the seams, and that they needed a little extra room around the belly.

So that was how Arvid and Jack first met, and over the next twenty years, when they came across each other in this mining camp or that, they'd laugh about that first shirt, maybe play a game of cards, and sometimes they'd partner up on the blacksmithing when there was a big job that needed to be done fast.

When they got Bo, they were both working at the Rampart mine on the Yukon.

The gold rush was all over, and most of those

thousands of early stampeders had quit the country when the big gold strikes played out.

Alaska was nearly empty again.

The stampeders left behind dozens of sad ghost towns—lonely stores with false fronts; abandoned old boats, paddle wheelers, rotting on sandbars; empty, echoing dance halls, their fancy oak floors and chandeliers thick with dust.

The ones who'd stayed, like the men at the Rampart mine, like Arvid and Jack, just stayed because the life pleased them, and because they loved the country.

So there they were at the Rampart mine together, Jack cooking after the regular cook took off, and everyone glad about it, because Jack was better than good at cooking.

And glad because the cookshack was always spotless when Jack ran it, with little things that made it home-like—maybe flowers on the table in the summer or a cloth on the long table.

That was because Jack had been raised in the kitchen of a big house down South, where Mama Nancy was in charge of the meals and housekeeping. She taught Jack to cook and keep things nice when he was a boy. The way Arvid had been taught sewing. Both very useful things for fathers, Bo always thought.

It'd been a bad year at Rampart. The gold was all played out, and Kovich, who owned the mine, was going to give it up after cleanup. He'd been a fair man to work for, and all the men were sorry he hadn't done well.

Rampart would be another ghost town.

All the miners at Rampart would be going out after cleanup. Some would take the boat upriver to Whitehorse so they could get the train and go down to the inland passageway to Seattle and home. They'd leave the country, and maybe they'd come back, and maybe they wouldn't.

Some of the men were headed to new diggings here and there. The mining on the Koyukuk was said to be looking good. Jack was going to the Koyukuk camp on the next steamboat going down the Yukon, and so was Arvid.

And that was why they got Bo. Because everyone in the camp knew they were headed downriver to Nulato. Everyone, including Mean Millie.

Jack just couldn't get over how amazing it all

was. If one tiny thing had been different, it wouldn't have happened. If they hadn't had to go to Nulato to wait for a scow going up the Koyukuk, if Arvid hadn't been standing outside when Mean Millie was getting on the steamboat, they wouldn't have had Bo. Just the littlest thing could change a life, he said, like someone bending down to tie a shoelace or someone getting a splinter. Little things that make other things happen. He called it thinking backwards.

Bo liked to think backwards like that a lot. "If I hadn't spilled my cocoa at breakfast, and if I hadn't taken so long to find the mop to clean it up, I wouldn't have been in the cookshack when the moose came to the window, and I wouldn't have seen him." The trouble was knowing when to stop. You could go backwards forever, like if there was no cookshack or no mining camp or if she'd never been born.

It could get really silly after a while.

CHAPTER TWO

BO COMES TO BALLARD CREEK

EVENING WAS BO'S favorite time of day, when Jack and Arvid were resting, the day's work all done.

This evening Bo was sitting at the long table with Arvid and Jack, cutting pictures out of old Montgomery Ward catalogs. Hank Redman was there too.

Hank was the new marshal. He had come to the cookshack after supper to pass some time with Jack and Arvid. He probably hoped Jack would have cake left over from supper, too. He was staying at the roadhouse, and Milo, the roadhouse man, wasn't famous for his cake.

Bo had heard all the grown-ups talking about how they liked the new marshal. Mostly it was because he didn't pay any attention to the stills. People around Ballard Creek made whiskey with stills since it was against the law to buy it.

Only trouble with making your own whiskey was that it took lots of sugar, and sugar was expensive. Sometimes, if it had been a long time before the scow came with groceries, there wasn't any sugar to be had at Milo's store. Bo knew making whiskey was kind of bothersome, because the grown-ups at Ballard Creek had a lot to say about it.

Hank Redman didn't seem to know there were such things as stills, and sometimes he'd even have a glass of whiskey with one of the good-time girls. Since nothing against the law ever happened in Ballard Creek except making whiskey, Arvid said Hank had a damned easy job.

While they talked, Bo cut out the tables and chairs and things from the furniture part of the catalog. Then she carefully pasted the cut-out furniture on

the inside of the shoe box
Jack had given her. That
would be the house for her
catalog people. She would cut
the people out last because they
were the hardest and sometimes
the scissors wouldn't behave, and her people ended
up without hands or feet. Maybe Jack would cut
them for her.

The paste jar had a little brush inside attached
to the lid, which she thought was a very good idea.
When no one was looking, she'd get some paste on
her finger and lick it off. It had a very interesting
taste. It tasted *white*.

New people like Hank didn't know everything
about everybody the way the people of Ballard
Creek and the mining camp did. New people were
always curious about Bo, which used to make her feel
cross.

"Just imagine," explained Jack. "Imagine someone seeing you for the first time with us two great big
men, one red-faced Swede and one black. Got to stir
up their curiosity. Would me!"

Hank was no different. He was curious, too.

When they'd stopped talking about Woodrow Wilson and Gene Tunney, the boxer, Hank nodded his head at Bo. "Tell me how you come to have this little one," he said.

Bo looked up at Hank. "My mama walked away. Like a turtle."

Arvid laughed. "It's a long story."

"Good," said Hank.

"Well, I can tell you the short version, or the long one," said Arvid.

Bo said, "Tell it all the way through."

Jack laughed and pinched her cheek. "Bo likes to hear us tell this, because she's the star of the story."

"Long is good," said Hank.

Arvid went to the stove and picked up the coffee-pot. "Anyone else?" Jack and Hank shook their heads, so Arvid poured the last of the coffee into his own cup. It was very thick and black. Arvid looked into the cup and said, "Maybe not," and put his cup down.

"Tell him," said Bo.

Arvid sat down at the table again.

"Well, we was at Rampart, me and Jack—1924, that was. Kovich'd just gone bust. You ever meet Kovich?"

Hank shook his head.

"Anyway," Arvid said, "after Kovich went belly-up, I wired up to the boss here at Ballard Creek to see if he had work. He did, sent me back a wire. Wanted a blacksmith, bad.

"Asked if any of the other men wanted work. Needed a cook, too, he said. I told the boys the next day when we was having breakfast, but they were all going to go upriver or someplace else when the mine closed.

"But Jack, he said he'd like to do that cooking job, so he wired the boss at Ballard here, and he got the job too. So me and Jack, we'd be leaving Rampart on the next boat going downriver.

"Now, this one day I'd just come off shift and went down to the riverbank to watch all the goings-on around the steamboat that just came in. The steamer *Clarice* it was. The deckhands were loading the wood. They made a long line, throwing logs from one to the other like they do, you know, and it was better than a show, watching them drop a log and getting all tangled up. I was laughing so hard I nearly choked."

"So there I was, leaning against the woodpile

down there at the riverbank, just watching all the hoorah, glad it wasn't me who had to get on that boat, go upriver, and quit the country. I rolled me a cigarette and was enjoying it, first one of the day, and watching Millie.

"Millie was one of the good-time girls, and she'd had a baby just a few weeks before. There she was with the bundle of baby, getting all her stuff put onboard the *Clarice*, hollering at the boys who were carrying her bags. A real witch, which was why everyone called her Mean Millie.

"When she was all finished yelling, she just walked up to me, where I was standing by the wood-pile, smoking and minding my own business, and pushed this baby at me. 'Take this kid to Nulato on

your way to the Koyukuk,' she said. 'The orphan-age there. I'm not going to be stuck with this baby forever.' "

"I just dropped my cigarette and took that baby. Never even thought to say no, because I didn't like Mean Milllie and didn't think no baby should be stuck with her, either."

Arvid said Millie sailed across the gangplank onto the boat and didn't look back. The boat edged out into the current and was on its way up the Yukon before Arvid really thought about what he'd done.

Then Jack told his part.

He'd been taking out the slop bucket when he first saw her. "I stopped dead in my tracks when I saw the Swede with that baby, looking up the river at the boat going away. I knew right off that was Mean Millie's baby. Only baby in camp. 'Got you a baby,' I says to him. 'I do,' says Arvid. 'What are you going to do with it?' I says. 'Damned if I know,' he says.

"So I took hold of her fast because I didn't like the way her head was bobbing around. Easy to see that Swede didn't know *nothing* about babies. 'We'll bring it in the cookshack,' I told him, 'and we'll study about it.'"

Bo had stopped pasting furniture so she could listen very hard.

"And what did you do then?" Bo asked, hugging her elbows and hunching her shoulders with excitement, as if she didn't know what was coming next.

"Well, I knew all about babies. Lots of babies in our kitchen when I was growing up down South. But first thing I thought of was a bottle. 'Millie got to have left you a bottle,' I said. Maybe she was nursing that baby the natural way, but it didn't seem likely. 'No,' says Arvid. 'Didn't leave me nothing.' 'Well, what's its name?' I ask. 'She never said.'

'Boy or girl,' I ask. He just looks at me and pulls his shoulders up. Doesn't know.

"So I get some old flour sacks from the shelf and some safety pins from the sewing box and I tell Arvid, 'First off we've got to change its pants. That's first.' So I show him how to fold the flour sacks small enough so the baby's legs won't stick straight out at the sides like a frog. And I take off that old saggy wet diaper, which was all her mama left her, and we look at each other. 'A girl,' we both say, and we smile. 'We'll call her Bo,' I said. 'Bo?' says Arvid. 'Bo,' I says."

"Why'd you pick Bo?" asked Bo, like she always did.

"It was a name was just sent to me, just popped into my head," which was what Jack always said. "I told the Swede, I said, 'Don't want to give her a real name—let them do that at the orphanage.' Give her a real name, and we'd maybe get attached to her. Like you don't want to give a stray dog a name, you know."

Hank lit his pipe and threw the match in the ashtray. He'd already figured out that Jack wouldn't take it kindly if he threw anything on the floor.

"I wouldn't have called her Bo," he said.

Jack ignored that.

"Arvid went out to look in Millie's cabin for a bottle, and sure enough, he found one, all scummed over. He washed it up, and already we had a bottle and plenty of milk in the cookshack and plenty of flour sacks for diapers.

"'She can sleep in this here tomato sauce box. You can take the night shift,' I says to Arvid, 'and I'll do the day.' 'Night shift?' he says. 'Babies don't sleep all the time,' I says. 'When they're awake, someone has to feed them and change them. That's the night shift for you, and I'll do the day.'

"'I can't take her to the bunkhouse,' says Arvid. 'The boys will have my hide.' 'We'll put a cot out for you right here, no trouble,' I tell him." Jack winked at Hank. "I knew he'd have *plenty* trouble, sleeping in that little short cot, but I didn't want to discourage him."

Jack leaned back in his chair and laced his fingers together behind his head, smiling. Bo could see he liked this story as much as she did.

"Next day Arvid was going to make her some clothes," Jack said, "some little long shift things on his sewing machine, but the only material he had was that striped twill he used for work shirts, too rough for a baby. So he made some little shifts out of our undershirts, nice and soft. We figured she'd need a lot more clothes than that, so he told the boys he'd give a dollar to anyone would give him their undershirts to make her some other things.

"But the boys wouldn't take any money for the undershirts because they were all tickled about her, glad to see her being cared for. Didn't call us seven kinds of fool, like we figured they would. They even started a collection at the saloon, brought us a bag of nuggets for her—wrote 'Bo' on the bag in fancy letters. 'That's her stake,' Kovich said."

"And tell him about how you kept me," Bo said. That was her favorite part.

"We went past the Ruby camp—used to be a big camp, but it was winding down by the time Bo was born. Past the Galena lead mines—all closed down, little town there, that's all—past the wood camps. Then a few hours before we got to Nulato, she looked up at us and she smiled, first time ever. This little crooked smile, just one-sided, funny as all hell, and we laughed so hard. 'Just like a real person,' Arvid said, like he'd never seen a baby smile before.

"Then we got off at Nulato, and we walked the little way to the Catholic church, where the orphanage was. We saw one of them nuns outside of the church—no one else, just her in this long black robe they wears, with a white cap thing, and by god, she looked mean. Mean as Mean Millie. We looked at her, and we just kept on walking to where we was going to catch the scow.

"We didn't say nothing, and then Arvid says, 'I think I'd like to call her Marta after my mother.' I says, 'That's a fine name.' And that was it. We never talked about it, never discussed nothing. We just made up our minds that we wasn't giving her to no one."

"Well," said Hank. He looked at Bo and shook his head in a wondering sort of way. "If that don't beat all."

Bo nodded with satisfaction. "Now tell him what everyone did when we got here," she said. That was her favorite part, too.

"Well," said Jack, "you never saw nothing like it. You'd a thought we'd brought a princess up the Koyukuk. Everybody, the whole town, was crazy about babies, which were few and far between. Eskimos are just foolish over babies. Then half the town is old bachelor miners, never had any babies of their own. They spoiled the Eskimo babies something awful. And here we come with a brand-new baby.

"Everyone in Ballard Creek hustled on down to

the riverbank when the bargemen yelled 'hoo hoo!' like they always do. We were on the first scow of the season, so the whole town was excited. Stopped work at the diggings even, to see who's coming, see what they brought. The kids mostly looking for candy. Always some candy on the first scow.

"So here are all these people—the whole town, the whole camp, down at the scow landing—and were they ever surprised to see Bo hanging over Arvid's shoulder, trying to lift her head up to see what all the noise was about.

"We stepped off the scow into this crowd, clapping their hands, the women holding their arms out for her. What a hoorah. And was she scared of all them people, hollering and carrying on, laughing fit

to die? Reaching to touch her? Not a bit. She smiled one of those sideways smiles again, and everyone went even crazier. Right there, she figured out that if she wanted everyone to go all goofy, all she had to do was take out that smile and there'd be all kinds of commotion. She was a big smiler from that time on."

Bo smiled at Hank to show him that was true.

" 'That's your baby?' They asked Arvid, because they knew right away couldn't be mine, black as I am," Jack said. 'It's *our* baby,' Arvid told them."

"And now here's the boss, meeting the scow, looking for me and the Swede. He walked right up to me and Arvid, shook our hands, and never blinked. Perfectly calm. Acted like he'd seen lots of drooling babies hanging over the shoulder of his new blacksmith. 'Lots of women here to help you with that,' was all he said."

"And there were, by god," said Arvid. "Women making her little Eskimo swing beds, and little parkas and boots, dance-hall girls knitting her blankets, couldn't do enough for her. And they're still doing for her." Arvid looked at Bo fondly. "When she got off that scow, it was just like she had a big family waiting for her."

Bo was happy. They'd told her story really well this time. Hank smiled back, shaking his head.

"Beats all," he said.

Jack jerked his chin at Bo. "Time you was in bed," he said.

Bo gathered her things together. She was supposed to do something right away, the first time they asked her, so she didn't argue, even though she had been wanting to ask Jack to cut the people out.

"Say good night to Hank," Arvid reminded her. Bo said good night and walked away from the table.

Then she stopped and looked back at Hank. "What would *you* have called me?" she asked.

Hank didn't even take time to think. "Would have called you Simone," he said. "I always liked that name."

CHAPTER THREE
IN THE COOKSHACK

BO STOOD in a slash of cool sunlight on a low
stool by the pastry table. The pastry table was
pushed up against the side wall of the cookshack,
the wall full of windows. She could see the whole
little sleeping town there over the creek, the dirty
snow half thawed, mud thick in the paths.

The miners got up long before anyone else was
awake in the town.

She was cutting out the biscuits. Her tongue
was sticking out, because you had to concentrate on
biscuits.

There were seventeen men to cook for, so that meant sixty biscuits to cut. That was her job every morning. When she was younger, Jack would mix the dough and roll them out for her, but now she was five and old enough to roll them out by herself.

Jack said biscuits were the most important thing a cook made and that you could tell right away what kind of cook you were dealing with when you saw his biscuits.

They had to be flaky, ready to fall apart almost, golden brown on top. You must never twist the cutter, or else they wouldn't rise up tall.

There were lots of other rules for making perfect biscuits, and Bo followed them all. She had taken on Jack's fussy ways, not Arvid's slapdash ways.

She cut the last biscuit and put it carefully on the baking sheet. You had to put them just so, far enough apart that they wouldn't bump into each other when they got bigger in the oven. If they touched, the sides wouldn't be crispy the way good biscuits had to be.

She wiped her hands on her apron and climbed off the stool. Jack was singing under his breath, a rumble from his broad chest, frying the potatoes in an enormous cast-iron skillet. Frying potatoes made a good brown smell.

She pulled at his apron. "Papa," she said, "they're ready."

He smiled down at her. "Just in time." He opened the huge oven door, and a wave of heat poured into the room. The oven had to be very hot to make biscuits. He put the pan on exactly the right rack, not too high and not too low, and closed the door.

Bo waited anxiously until it was time to take the biscuits out of the oven, because you could never be sure what kind of job you'd done until you saw them all baked.

Soon the kitchen was full of the good smell of biscuits. Jack took out the pan and set it on the side of the stove. Bo smiled. They were all standing tall, those biscuits, their flaky layers almost ready to tip over. Bo got a clean napkin from the drawer to line the tin washbasin they used for biscuits and then Jack slid all the biscuits off the pan into the basin. She looked a question at him and he nodded. She ran to the porch outside the cookhouse door and stood on her tiptoes to reach the iron triangle that hung from the porch roof. It was her job to call the miners to breakfast and lunch and dinner.

You had to take the little rod that hung with the triangle and bang it back and forth on the sides of the triangle. And you couldn't do it just once. You had to clang away for a long enough time that all the men in the bunkhouse would hear it, even if they were still asleep. She liked the noise the triangle made, bossy and loud.

And now in the spring, with the snow melting, it made an even bossier, louder sound. All the sounds seemed to be louder in the spring. You could hear things far away, even people chopping wood in the little town across the bridge.

She ran back inside the cookshack, banging the door, and carefully gathered up the pastry cloth she'd used to cut the biscuits on. She took it outdoors and shook the extra flour off of it, trying to be careful that none of the flour flew back on her. Then she folded the cloth carefully again and put it in its place in the pantry drawer. She wiped off the rolling pin and put it with the pastry cloth, and that job was done.

By that time, the porch was full of miners, some of them bending over the basins of water on the long bench by the door, throwing water on their faces to wake up, insulting each other.

"Shove over," Karl complained to Siwash George, and Peter growled at Dan, "You're getting more water on me than on yourself."

Bo loved to listen to them carry on. They were a good-natured bunch, Jack always said, but rowdy.

Then the cookshack was filled with the loudness of the men in their striped shirts and suspenders, their miners' boots noisy on the bare wood floor, and the clattering of the thick pottery.

Guillaume took Bo's hands and pretended to dance her down the room, singing "Casey Could Waltz with the Strawberry Blonde," because he always said that was the color of her hair. Well, strawberries were red, and her hair wasn't, so she didn't know why he said that. When Guillaume let her loose, Paddy pulled her braid and said, "Good morning, my darling."

Bo always got a little roughed up in the morning.

They took their bowls and plates from the table against the wall and sat at the long, long table, which was covered with oilcloth. Benches lined the sides of the table, and there was a chair for the boss at the head. Everyone had his own special place, though Bo didn't know how they'd decided it.

"In England," said Lester to no one in particular, helping himself to sausage, "the sausages are *much* fatter."

"Yeah, but we put meat in ours," Johnny said, which made everyone laugh.

What everyone called them, and what they called themselves, was "boys." "You boys move over," Dan said when Fritz and Andy were taking up too much room on the bench. The boys at the Ballard Creek mine, people would say, even if they were all pretty old. And Peter was very, very old.

They all had different ways of talking, because they came from different places. Bo was really good at imitating them. The boys would say, "Do Jack," and Bo would make her voice go all soft and slurry and slow like Jack's. "Do Sandor " they'd say, and she'd talk like Sandor, who was from a country called Hungary. The boys would laugh and slap their knees.

"Could be on the stage," Johnny always said.

Lester was the youngest, and Bo liked him very much. He had bright red hair, and his words bounced up and down. He said that was how they talked in London.

There was a place in London where people put on shows and sang songs and told jokes. The music hall. Lester taught her songs he'd learned there.

Bo's favorite music-hall song was "Don't Go in the Lion's Cage Tonight, Mother Darling, 'Cause the Lion Looks Ferocious and May Bite." It was about a circus lady who did tricks with lions. Bo knew it all the way through, and she and Lester would sing it at the roadhouse if someone asked them to.

Peter was the oldest miner. His eyes were pale blue and milky looking, and his hands had knotted veins all over them. But even if he was old, he was as strong as the other men.

Peter liked rocks. "Rocks are the oldest things on the earth," he'd told her. "They've been here since the beginning. Before any plants or animals. Before the oceans. They're *billions* of years old.

Bo had looked hard at Peter's kind face to see how old that was. Billions must be terribly old, but she couldn't even imagine being twelve or fifteen, so how could she think of billions? She couldn't *feel* what big numbers meant.

Peter taught Bo how to look for mica—the shiny stuff in rocks—and he would bring her any interesting rocks he found. Bo kept the rocks under the long table by the door in a Hills Bros. coffee can.

Bo's favorite rock was called schist. The mica in schist was streaked in long, shining lines straight across the rock, scraped there when the rock was under the earth and was being squeezed and stretched.

Peter complained about the rocks around the diggings. "Not of much interest," he said. "Other places in the world they have rocks full of crystals and sometimes bits of bugs or ferns from long ago. And some rocks that are made of nothing but ground-up shells. Those are really interesting, those kinds of rocks."

Bo wished she could see those shell rocks.

The boys teased him about his rocks. "Only rock I want to see is one with gold in it," they'd say.

Of the seventeen of them, of course Arvid and Jack were the biggest. Nobody was as big as they were. Karl was almost as tall as Jack and Arvid, but he was skinny. It would take two of his arms to make one of Jack's, Bo thought. Andy and Paddy were the shortest. Andy was square with stumpy legs, and Paddy was just a flimsy little man. "A rag and a bone and a hank of hair," was what Jack called him when he was teasing him.

Teasing was their favorite thing. They teased each other for being short, and they teased Jack and Arvid for being tall. They teased each other about their accents, they teased Lester for his red hair, and they teased Bo for being fussy like Jack. They teased Dan for eating fast, and they teased Sandor for snoring. They teased everyone in Ballard Creek for everything. They never stopped.

Jack had the table covered with a good breakfast. Besides the potatoes and the biscuits, there were bowls of honey and butter, platters of bacon and sausages and scrambled eggs, a big bowl of oatmeal to eat with canned milk and brown sugar, and tall stacks of sourdough hotcakes Jack had been keeping in the warming oven.

The boss liked to feed his crew well, because every day they all did hard, backbreaking work.

"Not a slacker among them," the boss used to say.

Arvid came banging through the cookshack door and took his place on the bench next to Bo at the end of the table. He was so big that when he sat on the bench, it sagged a little. He looked down at Bo.

"I beat you this morning," he said. "You were still snoring when I went to the shop."

"I do not snore," said Bo. "That's *you*."

The men passed around the plates and bowls of food and never stopped talking while they were eating. Jack said they were the talkingest bunch of men he'd ever worked with.

Except for the boss, that is. His name was Ed MacKay, but no one ever called him that, they just called him the boss. The boss never said much; he just looked quiet and calm, and when he had to talk, he said things in the shortest way possible.

Bo ate her stack of hotcakes with lots of syrup

and butter, and one biscuit with honey, and lots of potatoes, and two pieces of bacon. She was still hungry, so Arvid gave her one of his greasy sausages, which squeaked when she cut into it. She wasn't quite full yet, but she didn't want any oatmeal, so she and Arvid ate the last two biscuits, even though they were cold.

Jack was proud of the amount Bo could put away. "Just like one of the men," he said.

When they were finished and Jack was pouring out their coffee, little round Gitnoo burst in the door, slamming it against the wall like she always did. She came every morning to help Jack with the dishes and peel potatoes and do the piles of laundry in the washing shack. She was Ekok and Sammy's grandma, but she almost bounced she was so full of energy. When she laughed, her eyes squinted into half moons.

Gitnoo had never learned to speak English, so she told Bo what she wanted to say. Bo had learned to speak Eskimo right along with English.

Sometimes when the boys were teasing her or pulling her apron strings, Gitnoo told Bo to say naughty things to the miners. Bo knew you shouldn't say things like that in English, so Bo would just smile at Gitnoo and shake her head.

When Bo was first learning to talk, the Eskimo children taught her all the swear words in Eskimo and then would laugh until the tears ran down their faces to see their parents' mouths drop at such words coming from a very little girl.

Oscar was Bo's best friend. Oscar's mama, Clara, didn't think it was funny, and she made the kids stop teaching Bo such stuff. She told Bo not to say those words. Bo understood right away because Jack and Arvid had told her which of the English words she'd learned from the miners that she mustn't say. So she didn't say those words anymore when the grown-ups were listening. When the grown-ups weren't listening, all the children in Ballard Creek used all the swear words they knew, of course.

Bo could swear in Swedish, too, because that's what Arvid did. But Bo liked the Eskimo swear words the best because they felt all ragged in her throat.

After the boys had eaten their breakfast and Jack had poured their coffee, they lit up their pipes and the cookshack was filled with hazy smoke and the good smell of their tobacco. Then it was time for the boys to start work. They scraped back their chairs and benches and stretched. Alex and Sandor patted their round stomachs under their striped shirts.

"Your sourdoughs are going to kill me, and that's a fact," Sandor said to Jack.

They all said good-bye to Bo and piled their dishes on the table by the big sink for Gitnoo to wash, saying teasing things to her in English. They told her she was getting fat, or that she'd better save a dance for them next time at the roadhouse. Gitnoo laughed at them—she couldn't understand the words, but she could understand the meaning.

Then it was Bo's job to take the butter and syrup and other things on the table back into the pantry. After that, she must scrub the oilcloth that covered the long table.

Jack kept a spotless kitchen, and by the time she'd finished the table, he'd swept and mopped the floor. He did this after every meal. The miners' boots were always full of muck, especially now in the spring when the snow was melting. "Dirty floor makes me feel like my face is dirty," he'd say.

There was a big stack of dishes for Gitnoo to wash after every meal. Jack kept an eye on her to make sure she did it right. Gitnoo always put in so much soap that the bubbles floated away and fell in clumps on the floor. And sometimes she wouldn't get the water hot enough. The dishwashing water had to be very, very hot, and cups and silverware must be washed first. Jack had a lot of rules about washing dishes, and Gitnoo pretty much broke them all when he wasn't looking.

Gitnoo was singing loudly while she slammed the plates into the dishpan. She was like Jack, she loved to sing while she was working. She sang her special songs, the songs she'd made up. All the Eskimos made up songs—funny songs or sad or happy.

"What's that song about?" asked Jack.

Bo told him that Gitnoo's were all love songs about old boyfriends.

"Hmm," said Jack, looking at Bo suspiciously.

Bo knew he was worried that Gitnoo's love songs might not be okay for a little girl to hear. Eskimos talked about everything. They didn't think there were things they shouldn't talk about in front of children. The boys and the old-timers never talked about the things that the Eskimos talked about all the time.

When the table was finished, Bo took off her apron and put on Jack's big brown jersey gloves from the top of the wood box. It was her job every morning and night to bring in kindling and wood for the big stove and stack it neatly in the wood box.

Jack was the one who split the wood.

"Doing kitchen work, easy to get soft," he said. "If I didn't split wood every day, that Swede would be able to beat me at arm wrestling. And that's not a thing I could put up with."

Jack was very fussy about his wood. If you wanted a quick hot fire, like the kind you needed for biscuits or piecrust, that was birch, cut small. And for a slow fire, like you needed for beans or a moose roast, that was spruce. That's why the wood had to be carefully sorted so that he could put his hand on just what he needed.

Jack always bragged that Bo was a good worker because she filled up every section in the wood box right up to the top. "Bo never does anything halfway," he said.

If somebody praised you for doing a good job, you could never do it badly after that. Which Bo thought was kind of hard when she was feeling lazy.

CHAPTER FOUR
THE PEOPLE OF BALLARD CREEK

THE MINING CAMP was on one side of the creek, and on the other side were the cabins where the people of the town lived.

There was a little bridge over the creek, just past the cookshack, so you could go back and forth from the camp to the town without getting your feet wet.

Bo waded in the creek to get to town when she had her rubber boots on, and sometimes when she was barefoot. But not so often when she was barefoot because the water was bitterly cold.

"It wasn't very long ago," Arvid told Bo, "not

even thirty years, that there wasn't anything at all here—no town, no mining camp. Just the creek, all lonesome by itself."

Thirty years seemed to Bo like a long time, but Arvid said it was just a blink of the eye, really.

There were six old prospectors who lived in the town all year because they'd quit prospecting—too old to do the work. Everyone called them "the old-timers."

Sol was the old-timer who told Bo and Oscar the best stories about the old days in Ballard Creek. He had been there from the beginning, since the stampede.

"What's a stampede?" Bo had asked Sol.

"A stampede is when a whole lot of people rush to someplace to find gold," Sol told them. "Craziness, really, that's what a stampede is."

Sol and his partner, along with hundreds of other prospectors, came swarming up the Koyukuk because they'd heard there was a big gold strike on the river.

"A hundred rickety cabins popped up, the kind a couple of men can build in a day or two. And there it was, almost overnight, a new little town right in the middle of the tundra. They built so many cabins that they used up all the spruce trees for miles around. You know how far you and your dad got to go to cut wood, Oscar. Well, back at the beginning, you could have cut wood outside your front door, there was so many trees."

"Too bad," said Oscar when he'd thought that over. "They were too greedy for trees."

"Stampeders don't exactly worry about what they'll leave behind," said Sol. "Just one thing on their mind: getting rich."

Pictures of that stampede time were pinned up on the road-house wall. In the pictures, there were lots of white tents besides the cabins Sol told them about, and stacks and stacks of firewood piled next to every cabin or tent.

The tents had signs on them that Milo, the road-house man, read for them: LAUNDRY DONE HERE; SMOKEY'S RESTAURANT; HAIRCUTS, TWO BITS.

Most of the stampeders partnered up so they could look after each other, help each other out. Sol's partner in those days was Harry Ballard.

"He was a good partner," Sol told Bo and Oscar. "Talked all the time, but that was okay. Made up for me. I never have much to say." Sol looked sadly at his gnarled old hands. "Killed by a bear right there on that creek, Harry, almost on the spot where the bridge is."

Bo's eyes stretched wide, trying to imagine a bear crunching on her bones.

"Was you with him when the bear got him?" Oscar asked.

"No, he was prospecting on his own while I was out at our claim, digging a shaft. What we found was big prints and some little ones, mama bear with cubs. Harry, he had real bad eyes. Started out on the Klondike with some glasses, but lost those early. The way I figure it, he didn't see the bear. Didn't see she had cubs.

The stampeders named the creek Ballard Creek

to remember him by, and the town was named Ballard Creek as well. "I think Harry would have thought it was something to have a creek and a town named for him," Sol said.

"And did the stampeders get rich, Sol?" Bo asked.

"Nah, like to nearly starved that winter. Couldn't find the gold they wanted, so as soon as spring came, they rushed up to Nome to the new gold strike there, the whole kit and kaboodle."

"Whole kit and kaboodle," Oscar and Bo said to each other, pleased with the way it sounded. "Kit and kaboodle."

"Whoosh, those men were gone! Overnight!" said Sol. "Treading on each other's heels, afraid someone would beat them to the new strike."

Bo could just see them in her head, pushing each other, just like the kids when there was candy at the roadhouse.

"And almost all the little houses were left empty," said Sol. "A hundred empty houses is a sight to see."

"Why did you stay, Sol?" Oscar asked.

"I just liked it here, soon as I came. Married me an Eskimo girl. We had a little boy."

Bo looked hard at Sol. She knew he lived alone

now. Sol nodded at the question she didn't ask. "Died of the diptheria, both of them," he said.

"I know that," said Oscar. "That was my mama's aunt you was married to."

"Right," said Sol. "That's how come they call me uncle, still look after me some. Eskimos is big on family."

But the little houses didn't stay empty. Sol said while the stampeders were coming and going, a lot more Eskimos from the coast by Kotzebue came down the Kobuk River. They wanted a new place to live with better hunting, more room.

"Right away they settled into the empty cabins and burned the extra ones for firewood. So now we got nine, ten Eskimo families and plenty of kids."

"Fifteen kids," said Oscar. "There's eleven in school. Me and Bo and Evalina and Kapuk—we're the only ones not in school. So that's fifteen."

"Lucky for you, Bo," Sol said. "Most mining camps I ever seen didn't have any children at all."

And it *was* lucky because of Oscar—smiling, happy, Oscar. Bo and Oscar had played together since they were babies.

Arvid and Jack used to tease Bo about the way she'd pulled Oscar's long black shock of hair when she couldn't even walk yet. Even though Oscar was a little older than Bo, Bo was bigger than he was.

But Oscar didn't mind that Bo was bigger. He was too happy-go-lucky to mind anything.

SO NOW THERE WERE about thirty little cabins scattered higgledy-piggledy along the dusty, rutted paths, and all of them had windows that looked out onto the Koyukuk River.

Milo's roadhouse was right in the middle of town, and it was the only building with two stories. There was a little school cabin and a tiny house for the wireless, where people sent telegraphs, and next to that was the tall wireless tower. There was a big old building that used to be a dance hall, but the windows were boarded over because they didn't need a room that big for dances anymore. All the dancing was at the roadhouse.

And this was who lived in Ballard Creek: the Eskimos and the old-timers, the boys from the mine, Milo at the roadhouse, the good-time girls, Lilly and Yovela, and in the winter, Miss Sylvia, the teacher.

Bo and Oscar and the other children had a busy time visiting all of them.

The miners who had claims on the creeks outside the town would walk into town whenever there was something going on, like the Fourth of July or Christmas, or just whenever they got lonesome out at their claims. Sometimes they walked in—ten, twenty, thirty miles—just because they wanted to dance.

There was always dancing at Ballard Creek. All someone had to do was ring the bell at the roadhouse, and everyone in town would come to dance.

Jack used to brag about them. "The people of Ballard Creek are the dancingest people I ever heard tell of. And the walkingest," he said.

CHAPTER FIVE
AT OSCAR'S HOUSE

THE DAYS GREW warmer and warmer. Pools and puddles were everywhere as the winter snow disappeared. When Bo went to visit Oscar, all the snow on the roof of Oscar's cabin was dripping into the soft tired snow around the house. The snow was grainy and didn't glitter in the sun. Soon it would be all melted away.

Oscar's mother was Clara, and she was always glad to see Bo. "*Onee, onee,*" she cried happily—come in. Bo thought she was very pretty with her shiny black hair pulled back into a bun.

"Oscar, he's getting water," said Clara. "Be right back."

Clara was like Jack, always working. She was sitting on her woven grass sewing mat on the splintery lumber floor, her legs straight out in front of her, the way Eskimo women always sat.

She was patching Oscar's winter mukluks. "He can wear them another year if I put a new sole on them," she said. "Still good. Oscar, he takes good care of his things."

Clara talked around the stem of the long pipe she was smoking, little curls of smoke going up into the air in the slant of bright spring sunlight that came in the window.

Lena, Oscar's big sister, was playing her favorite record on the Victrola: "Bye-Bye, Blackbird." She grabbed Bo's arms and danced her gaily around the room. "Pack up all your cares and woes, here I go, singing low, bye-bye, blackbird," she sang. Bo laughed at Lena. Lena was the kind of person who always made you laugh.

"Sit down here, you bad girl," Clara said to Lena. "You got to twist this sinew for me, not be dancing all the time!" But she wasn't really cross. Eskimos were never cross with their children.

Nearly every house in Ballard Creek had a Victrola, and nearly everyone had a good stack of records to play. You had to wind up the little brass handle on the Victrola after you'd put the record on the round turntable and set the arm with the needle down on the first groove of the record. When the winding began to run down, the song would grow lower and slower and start to growl before it quit entirely. Lena dashed to the Victrola and wound it up again as soon as the song started to drag.

Clara sighed. "Same song, too many times."

The walls of Oscar's house were covered with yellow oilcloth, and Lena had decorated the walls with pictures she'd cut out of magazines. She stuck them on the wall with flour-and-water paste. The pictures were mostly of pretty girls she'd cut from the yellow *National Geographic*s Sol Evans gave her when everyone was finished with them. They were girls from other countries with different kinds of clothes on.

And there was one picture of a camel. He had an angry face. Lena thought that was very funny and liked to make mean faces back at the camel. "Good thing our moose aren't so grumpy," she said.

There were two spruce-pole bunks against the wall, with fat ticking mattresses full of dried grass from the grass lakes. That was where Lena and Oscar and their brother, Peluk, slept. Peluk had gone hunting that morning with Oxadak, Oscar's father. Nobody expected them to come back with anything.

"Bad time, spring," Clara said. "Hard to find food. No fish, no birds, no game, can't walk on the rotten snow. Used to be the starving time; people died then. Now we got the store, got clams to make chowder and milk for the babies, but it's not the same as our meat. We got to have meat, or we don't feel right."

Oscar came in, sloshing water from his bucket onto the floor.

He threw his mother a sorry look.

"You're in too big a hurry. You know Bo is here," said Clara. Oscar smiled his big smile, the smile that squeezed his black eyes nearly shut.

"Good you come!" he said. "Nakuchluk's making akutaq for Sammy's birthday!"

Akutaq was everyone's favorite thing. The boys and the old-timers called it Eskimo ice cream, even if there wasn't any ice or any cream in it, like the ice cream Jack made sometimes in the winter when there was ice. Akutaq was made from caribou bone marrow and fat all melted together. It was a lot of work, because you had to whip all the marrow and fat with your hands until it was fluffy as a cloud. Then you put in berries, and the akutaq turned a beautiful pink color.

Bo had asked Jack to make akutaq, but he just raised his eyebrow at her. Akutaq, he said, was the sort of thing you had to be raised with to like. Same as stinkfish. And seal oil.

"And olives," Bo had said.

Bo loved akutaq as much as Oscar did.

"Let's go see if it's ready!" she said.

"You bring me back a little dish of it," said Clara.

"I'm going with you," said Lena. "I want a big dish!"

"First you finish that sinew," said Clara. Oscar wiped up the water he'd spilled and said, "We'll go just as soon as I get the wood."

Oscar had to fill the wood box just like Bo did,

but Clara wasn't as fussy about her wood as Jack was, and Oscar only had to cut a pile of kindling and bring in enough spruce for the day. Oscar had a little ax and was allowed to cut the kindling. Bo wasn't allowed near an ax. She couldn't wait until she could cut wood like all the older children.

Lena sat on the floor with her mother and began twisting the sinew that was used for sewing thread. Sinew made strong, almost invisible stitches and never rotted like the store-bought thread. It came from the hump on the back of the caribou, but the muscle fibers were short. They had to be twisted together into long threads for sewing.

Bo sat down next to Lena. She didn't like to stretch her legs out like they did. It made the back of her knees feel funny. So she sat with her legs folded under her.

Lena took two short pieces of sinew and rubbed the ends together between her palms until the ends were twisted together and it was a long piece. Lena took two more pieces of sinew and gave them to Bo. "You try it." Bo tried, but her hands were clumsy and the pieces didn't twist together.

"Easier if you start with leg sinew—that's thicker,"
said Clara. Bo smiled at her. Clara always made an
excuse for you if you made a mistake or couldn't do
something well.

"This caribou hump makes the thinnest thread—
best for fancy sewing, but harder to twist."

Clara and all the other Eskimo mamas had

sewed for Bo along with all their other sewing—
winter mukluks and summer moccasins, caribou
parkas for cold, cold winter, big fur mittens.

Then Arvid would make something on his sewing machine in return, to pay for the things they'd
made for Bo—calico parka covers, overalls like Bo's
for the kids. Even the big boys and girls liked Arvid's
overalls. It was a good system, trading work.

WHEN OSCAR had finished with the wood and they
were going out the door, Clara called them back.

"Here, take these to Milo on your way," she said,
handing Oscar a pile of magazines.

Most of the people who lived in Ballard Creek
subscribed to at least one magazine, and when they
were finished reading them, they'd take them to the
roadhouse for everyone else to read. So there were a
lot of magazines to keep up with.

All the children in Ballard Creek went to the
roadhouse nearly every day to read magazines, sitting on the floor with their backs against the wall,
feet sticking straight out. The good thing for Bo and
Oscar was that someone was always there to read
the captions of the pictures to them. They were the

only children in Ballard Creek besides Evalina and Kapuk, Dishoo's baby, who couldn't read.

The yellow *National Geographic*s were the ones all the children liked best. The old-timers and the miners liked the scientific magazines the best. They had lots of new inventions in them. The men in Ballard Creek used to get more excited about new inventions than almost anything else.

The miners who lived out at the creeks would take loads of magazines out to their claims and bring them back in their rucksacks or at the bottom of a sled. After all this borrowing and going back and forth, all the magazines looked pretty shabby, and some of them didn't have covers. But no one ever threw them away.

Milo always said magazines in Ballard Creek had nine lives.

CHAPTER SIX

AT THE ROADHOUSE

WHEN BO AND OSCAR went into the roadhouse with Clara's magazines, Milo was making a new pot of coffee in the big percolator.

Milo was a short, square man from Yugoslavia. He had a huge head of gray hair, and he always wore a dirty dish towel wrapped around his middle.

His coffeepot was dirty, too—black and greasy, not shiny like Jack's.

Some of the old-timers, Jimmy the Pirate and Tomas and Ollie Deglar, were there as usual, drinking coffee. They were retired and had time to drink coffee all day if they wanted.

They bragged that Milo made the worst coffee on the Koyukuk, and only strong men like them could drink it and live. Bo and Oscar had tried some once, and it certainly was terrible.

Dinuk, who was Jonas's papa, and Unakserak, who was Nakuchluk's old husband, were there too, playing cribbage. They didn't like coffee.

"Here's Bad Oscar and his sidekick Bo," Milo said when they came in together. That was what he always said. "What are you two outlaws up to today?"

"Up to no good," said Jimmy the Pirate. They called him that because he had only one eye. Sometimes he wore a black eye patch over his bad eye, but sometimes he didn't. His bad eye was very interesting, milky and twisted, the lid red and angry looking.

"Akutaq today," said Bo. "Nakuchluk is making it."

Ollie made a gagging face to show what he thought of akutaq, and Bo laughed.

"You kids don't go around the river today," said Jimmy. "Ice breaking up. Water might come up fast."

"We know," said Bo.

Oscar held out the magazines his mother had given him. "Ma says thank you," he said to Milo.

Cannibal Ivan came into the roadhouse looking grumpy. He was called Cannibal because he liked his meat just barely cooked, pink all through. He never got it that way at Milo's, though he complained about it.

"Rheumatism kept me up all night," he said, pulling up a chair. "Getting old."

Bo looked at Cannibal carefully. "I thought you were already old," she said.

Cannibal ignored that. "Well, don't just stand there," he said to Bo and Oscar. "Sit down and have a cup of coffee with us,"

Bo and Oscar smiled at him. "I hate coffee," Oscar said.

Jimmy leaned forward and looked at Oscar

seriously. "That's why you don't have no whiskers yet," he said.

THERE WERE A LOT of good things to do at the roadhouse besides reading magazines. Milo had a big fancy iron coffee mill that stood on the floor next to the big woodstove. Milo let any of the children who were handy turn the crank to grind the coffee beans into powder. It wasn't hard, and the coffee smelled good.

Bo wished coffee tasted like it smelled.

The bar stools were another good thing. They were left over from the old days when people sat at the bar to drink whiskey. Before there was the law about whiskey. Those stools would spin around in a circle. The children took turns spinning each other until they were dizzy.

And there were two big brass spittoons at either end of the bar. Spittoons were for people who didn't set their tobacco on fire. They chewed their tobacco, and when they were finished with it, they needed a place to spit it out. That was what a spittoon was for.

No one in Ballard Creek chewed their tobacco anymore, but Milo kept the spittoons. He said you never could tell when someone would come in who needed one. And you certainly didn't want to have people who chewed left on their own without a spittoon—couldn't tell where they'd let fly.

What the Ballard Creek kids liked about the spittoons was that you could see yourself in them. Not your real self, but a shiny gold self with a big fat nose and weird eyes and all sorts of funny mouths, depending on how far you stood away and how you made your faces.

Making faces in the spittoons was one of their favorite things.

The roadhouse was a long building, and it had to be because it was used for so many things.

In one corner was Milo's little store, where he sold everything—canned food and dried beans, sugar and salt, 30-30 shells, tobacco, Pilot Bread crackers, tea. Sometimes Bo would dust all the tops of the cans and set them up in neat rows after everyone had messed things up.

When the scow came in, there were American cheese and eggs, onions and sometimes oranges. But they didn't last long, because when the scow came in with fresh food, people would pile up at the store counter in the roadhouse, pushing each other a little, and before long, it was all sold.

But Milo always saved exactly fifteen oranges, enough for every child in town. He'd write their names on the bumpy skin with a grease pencil so he wouldn't leave anyone out or give two to the same person: Ekok, Sammy, Manuluk, Jonas, Johnny, Della, Atok, Peluk, Kapuk, Evalina, Oscar, Lena, Annie, Betty, and Bo.

Lots of times, people couldn't pay for their groceries, but Milo would just write their names in the book on the counter, and they'd pay when they had some money or when they brought in something to sell, like furs in the winter or dried fish in the fall, or maybe fresh caribou or sheep meat after they'd been hunting.

When Jack sent Bo to the store for something,

Milo always opened that green book with red leather corners and found the page that said Ballard Mining Company. Then he'd tell Bo to sign her name next to the list of things she bought. She could write a really lumpy *o*, but her *B* always went wrong.

"Is that right?" she'd ask Milo.

"Backwards again," he'd say. "Better luck next time."

Upstairs there were six rooms for overnight visitors. That was where the game warden, Sam White, stayed when he came to town, and the mail carriers, and the marshal, Hank.

In the winter, it was very cold upstairs. Everyone who stayed there said they could see their breath. But in the summer, it was incredibly hot up there, so Milo said it evened out.

Those six rooms were pretty dusty and not noticeably clean. But nobody who came to the road-house was fussy.

BO AND OSCAR and Jimmy the Pirate watched Unakserak and Dinuk play cribbage for a while. Bo thought it looked like fun, but there was too much counting. Counting was not one of her best things.

"My wife liked to play cribbage," said Jimmy. "She always cheated."

Bo looked at Jimmy with surprise. None of the old-timers had wives.

"Where *is* your wife, Jimmy?" she said.

"Oh, I kind of lost track of her," Jimmy said, and winked at Milo.

Bo hadn't known you could lose track of wives.

JACK WAS SHAVING and Arvid was putting wood in the fire for the night, and they both stopped what they were doing and looked at Bo when she said, "Did you lose track of your wives?"

"Wives?" said Jack, in his are-you-crazy voice. "What wives?"

"Jimmy the Pirate had a wife, and he lost track of her," Bo explained.

"Ohhh," Jack said, trying not to smile. "What Jimmy meant," he began, and then stopped, looking as if he didn't know what to say next.

"What Jimmy meant," Arvid said, "is that his wife walked away, or he walked away—you know, like your mama. People who are married don't always stay together."

"Well," said Bo, "did you have wives?"

"No," said Arvid, "we never had any wives, me and Jack."

"Why not?" said Bo.

"Well, for my part, no one ever asked to marry me," said Arvid with his biggest smile. "And a good thing, too," he said.

Bo felt that there was something wrong with that answer, so she looked at Jack, who had gone back to shaving.

"I was going to get married, when I was real young, back home," Jack said. He wiped the soap off his face with the towel.

"Nellie, that was her name. She died of the fever, same time as Mama Nancy."

Bo stood still. A lot had happened to her papas before they got her. It made her feel funny. She pulled her pajama top over her head and bent down to put her slippers on.

Then she looked up into Jack's face and said, "Was she nice?"

Jack smiled and nodded.

"Was she pretty?" Bo asked.

"People you love are always pretty," said Jack.

And Bo knew that was true.

CHAPTER SEVEN

BEAUTY PARLOR

AFTER THE ICE had gone out and the river was clear, tiny leaves came out on the birch trees and the aspens. The new leaves looked like a pale green mist all over the far hills across the river. The snow had gone except for in little hollows where it had lain very deep and under the spruce trees where the shadows stayed all day. Mud had taken its place. It would be a long time before it dried up.

When Bo went to town, she'd decide who to visit first, depending on what time it was—early in the morning, or afternoon—rain or sunshine. Oscar usually went visiting with her, but this morning he was out in the woods behind town cutting wood with his father.

Bo decided she'd visit Lilly or Yovela. Maybe Yovela. Lilly liked to sleep late, but Yovella'd be up.

Everyone called Lilly and Yovela "the good-time girls," or sometimes "the sporting girls." Jack told her that was because when Lilly and Yovela were young, they'd worked at the dance hall when the town was full of stampeders, and dance-hall girls were there so you could have a good time. And *sporting* meant the same thing, having a good time. The rest of the good-time girls had gone way before Bo came along, but Lilly and Yovela stayed.

Yovela was dark and plump and round, with deep dimples in her face and shining black eyes. She always wore long dangling earrings that made little noises when she shook her head.

Lilly had blue eyes and long blond hair that she twisted on top of her head. Into the twist she put shiny combs with jewels in them. She said she got her hair out of a bottle, but Bo didn't know what that meant.

Bo wore overalls every day, the kind that

buttoned over her shoulder. Arvid made them out of blue denim or out of the blue-striped twill the miners used for their shirts. In the winter, she had woolen long johns under the overalls, and wool sweaters over them. When it got to be summer, she could take off the long johns, and then she wore just the overalls and little flannel shirts that Arvid made, too.

Lilly and Yovela hated to see Bo dressed like a boy. So they made her dresses like they did for the other girls in town. They liked to sew.

When Bo went to a dance, she always wore one of the dresses. Lilly and Yovela didn't like it that Bo wore her heavy leather shoe packs with the dresses, or the moccasins the Eskimo mamas made her. They said she should have proper shoes to wear with a dress.

Yovela showed Bo a picture of herself when she was a little girl. She was wearing little shiny high black boots, with lots of buttons on them. Yovela said you had to have a special tool to button those buttons. Bo was very happy that she didn't have to wear any such thing.

It was Lilly who made Bo's bear, when Bo first

started walking. Lilly dyed some
white drill cloth with tea to make it
brown. She cut the bear out of that
and sewed it up with scraps of cloth for
stuffing, and embroidered round black eyes
and a nose and a mouth. It had sharp ears like a fox,
not round like a bear, so people used to tease Lilly
that she must have gotten her animals mixed up.

But Bo liked his ears just fine and hardly ever
went anywhere without that bear. At night, he slept
in the little cradle Sandor had made for her when
she was a baby.

She called him Bear.

"Ought to name him," said Jack from time to
time.

"I'm waiting for a name to come to me, like you
found the name Bo," she always said.

Bear got very beat up in his life with Bo, so Lilly
had to take the stuffing out of Bear every year and
wash him and redye him with tea. Once she put
buttons on for eyes after she'd washed Bear, but he
looked so different with buttons that Bo cried and
Lilly had to take them off.

◆◇◆◇◆

BO AND ALL the other children liked to visit the good-time girls because their cabins were so fancy. Especially Yovela's.

You had to take your shoes off in Yovela's porch so you wouldn't track in dirt when you went into the cabin. Yovela's board floors were painted and shiny, and there was a flowered rug right in the middle of the floor.

As soon as you opened the door, you smelled Yovela's special smell. It didn't smell like slop bucket or cooking, like everyone else's cabin. It was her perfume, Eau de Gardenias, which she kept in a little glass bottle with a rubber pump on top. It was very expensive, and you couldn't play with that bottle, but once in a while, she would squirt a little on Bo. When she went back home, Jack would take a sniff and say, "Been visiting Yovela, huh?" because Yovela was the only one who ever smelled like that.

Yovela's big bed had olive green silk pillows that matched the coverlet. Propped in the middle of the pillows was a beautiful doll, dressed in the fanciest dress you could ever imagine. Bo always put Bear up there so Bear and the doll could talk.

Once Bo had jumped up on that bed and one of

the mattress coils that was broken and sticking out had cut her leg badly, and she had bled all over Yovela's rug. Yovela got the blood out of the rug, but Bo still had the scar. After that, the children were not allowed to climb up on the bed, ever.

Yovela had lots of records, and she'd always let the children play whatever they wanted. She had one called "Who Takes Care of the Caretaker's Daughter When the Caretaker's Busy Taking Care?" You had to sing that very fast, so all the words ran together. That was Bo's favorite at Yovela's.

Yovela was happy to see her, as she always was, and she showed Bo her new magazines and let Bo play her favorite record. But while Bo was listening, Yovela came behind her and picked up Bo's braids in a thoughtful kind of way.

Bo's heart sank. Sometimes Yovela took a notion to play "beauty parlor" with the girls. That's what she called it. She'd fix their hair with ribbons or flowers and combs, put rouge on their faces, and screw a pair of her long earrings onto their earlobes. The big girls, like Della and Lena, Oscar's sister, and the twins Annie and Betty, loved to play beauty parlor. Bo hated it.

But Bo was the only one with long hair. The other girls—even the little ones—had their hair cut short like the women in the catalogs. So Yovela liked playing with Bo's hair the best.

"Bo, let me fix your hair nice," Yovela said.

Bo could only look at her. Yovela didn't seem to notice that Bo was feeling unhappy.

She took Bo's hair out of its braids, and then she made her bend over the wash bowl while she washed her hair with some perfumey soap and then toweled it almost dry. She rubbed it so hard that Bo's breath was coming in gasps.

Then Yovela made Bo sit still on the chair by the table while she brushed her damp hair out straight. Then she wound up fat round curls, which she tied with her curling rags until Bo's head was full of little packages of curls tied in bows.

"Now we'll have some tea and Melba toast and wait for them to dry," she said in a pleased way. "It's going to look so beautiful."

So she made the tea in the fancy little pot Bo and the other girls liked so much and put the toasts on a plate with roses on it. But Bo couldn't enjoy the pretty pot or the roses. Yovela chattered about hair.

She thought the new fashions with short hair were terrible and Bo should never think of it.

"A woman's hair is her glory," she said. "When I was a little girl, I had scarlet fever, and they cut all my hair off. That's what they used to do in those days to help you get well. I cried and cried when I saw my head covered with prickles. My mother said, 'Don't cry, Emma. It will grow back,' and it did, but it took so very, very long."

Bo looked up quickly when Yovela said that.

"Why did your mother call you Emma?" she said.

Yovela laughed. "That's my real name," she said. "I just thought it was too plain, so when I left home I called myself Yovela. Don't you think it's a pretty name?"

Bo did, but she asked, "Was your mama sad that you changed your name?" Yovela picked up her cup and looked into it. "My mother died before my hair grew out," she said.

When Yovela thought the curls were dry enough, she untied each one and then brushed it out, wrapping it around her finger, and placed each long corkscrew carefully on Bo's shoulder.

"There! You're a picture." She held up her fancy gold mirror to Bo. When Bo looked in the mirror, she bit her lip and scowled horribly.

"What a face!" cried Yovela. "Don't you like it?"

Bo threw a despairing look at Yovela and backed away from the mirror. "I have to go." She took Bear off the bed and tried not to run out the door.

"Well, wait," Yovela protested. "Here's some chocolates for you. I saved them from my last box." Bo took one of the chocolates to be polite and then she turned and ran.

Bo ran all the way through town. She ducked into the bushes when Peluk, Oscar's brother, pumped by on his bicycle, and she dashed across the bridge. She stomped into the cookshack and was happy that Jack wasn't there to see the miserable curls, bobbing and bouncing on her shoulders.

She grabbed the brush she shared with Arvid and Jack, not that they needed it much. Jack had a shiny bald spot on top of his head and lots of curls fluffed out around his ears, and Arvid, whose hair was straight and thick, kept his cropped very short and it sort of stuck up in porcupine tufts.

Bo yanked at those curls with the brush, but they bounced back like springs, so she went outside to the rain barrel and dumped a dipper of water over her head. She bent over to wring her hair out, and just then, Jack came around the corner from the storage shack. He raised his eyebrows, asking a question. Jack never used any words he didn't have to.

"Yovela made me curly again," she said, facing him with water dripping down her face.

Jack smiled broadly. "I recollect how you hated it the first time she did that to you. Must have been two years ago." He led her into the cookshack and got a towel to dry her hair.

"Guess you're not going to be a girlie girl," he said. He brushed her hair out straight and did her braids up. "Maybe if you had a mama, or sisters, you might have gone that way. Too late now, I guess."

"Well, you don't like it either, all that curly mess," said Bo, scowling at him.

"Hah, I guess not. I like things to be just what they is. No messing with them."

"Right," said Bo. "Me too."

"You could tell Yovela that," said Jack.

"But Lilly and Yovela, they're so fancy," Bo wailed. "They don't leave nothing the way it is. They're just always cranking in those corsets and shining their nails and doing their hair."

"Well," said Jack, "that's kind of like their job. That's why they call them fancy women, some places."

"I might hurt their feelings if I said I didn't want to be like that." Bo said.

"That's true," said Jack. "Guess you don't have any better friends than Yovela and Lilly. But you know, you just tell them in a nice way, tell them you don't want to be fancy. You just want to be Bo. They'll understand."

"Well, I'm not going to visit her anymore," said Bo. "Not unless Oscar is with me."

CHAPTER EIGHT

SURPRISE FOR OLLIE'S BIRTHDAY

OLLIE DEGLAR was having a birthday party at the roadhouse. Everyone in town was going to be there. Jack had made a big cake for him, and now that the chores were done and the cookshack was spotless, Jack was ready to decorate it.

Jack made cakes for everyone's birthday. He had a special little kit of colors to dye the frosting and canvas tubes to squeeze the frosting out in lines. Bo would never miss watching Jack make one of his cakes.

She liked to watch him get ideas. His gray eyes got a sort of still, quiet look as if he was waiting. Bo could see that ideas were things that just popped into your head if you waited. Like magic. But Jack could never tell her how it happened.

"Just come to me," he'd say.

Bo tried to watch herself get ideas, but it was like trying to catch a butterfly.

Every cake was something special. A round cake for Yovela looked like a hat with frosting feathers, almost like the one Yovela wore to be very fancy. He made a rainbow cake for Manuluk last year when she turned ten. He cut a round cake in half and stood both halves up on the plate on their cut ends to make the bow, and then frosted the bow with the different colors of the rainbow.

"Rainbow colors have to go in a certain order," Jack told Bo. "You can't put the colors any old way. "Red, orange, yellow, green, blue, violet," he said. "That's the way they go. Fix that in your mind."

Manuluk loved that cake so much she cried when her mother cut into it. Jack gave Manuluk a big hug and told her not to worry—he'd make her a rainbow cake every year if she wanted, so Manuluk stopped crying and ate two pieces herself.

Ollie was a plain sort of person, so Ollie's cake was not fancy. Jack made a long chocolate cake with a shorter cake on top so that the two layers made a kind of step.

He slathered both cakes with frosting and then he put white frosting in his canvas tube for decorating. This was the part Bo liked to watch the most. Jack wrote Ollie's name on top of the cake in big white frosting letters and then some numbers: 1859 and 1929.

"What are those numbers?" Bo asked.

"That is the year Ollie was born, and that's the year today," Jack said.

"That's how it is on the grave markers down in the burial place. Two sets of numbers," Bo said thoughtfully.

Jack looked at her with a funny expression.

"That's so," he said. "That's so." He twisted his mouth in his thinking way.

"I think I won't use these numbers." Jack took his big knife and swiped off the writing on the top of the cake. "Don't want the cake to look like a gravestone."

"How did you know when Ollie was born?"

"I asked him," said Jack. "The thing about old people is, no one asks them enough questions. They get to thinking no one is interested. Said he was going to be seventy, so that's 1859. That's subtraction. When you get to school, you'll see how it works."

Jack frowned at the cake. "Now what?" he said. Bo watched Jack's face intently, trying to see the moment he got an idea, and where it came from. He scowled some more and twisted his mouth, and suddenly his frown went away.

"Bring me the atlas, Bo."

Bo knew that was the big book with maps in it, because the miners used it a lot. Most of the time, they got the atlas when they were arguing about something. The atlas was to prove who was right about something, like the time that Lester said that London was on the same line as Sitka, and Paddy said he was crazy, it was no such thing, and they got out the atlas and Paddy was right.

She didn't know what Jack wanted the atlas for, but she didn't ask, because in a few minutes she'd know. Jack always said don't ask questions when there's an emergency, and don't ask questions if you're going to find out right away by watching.

Bo pulled the atlas out of its place on the shelf and hugged it to her chest as she carried it to Jack because it was very heavy. She dropped it on the table with a thump. Jack turned to a page in the middle that showed all the flags of the countries.

"Norway," he said, running his big finger down the page. "That's where Ollie was born. Here's what I was looking for. That's the flag of Norway. That would look good on the cake, wouldn't it? Not too hard to do." Bo could see right away what a good idea that was. But she wished she knew where the idea had come from.

Jack stared at the cake again.

He mixed a little red color into some of the white frosting and then he made some blue. The Norwegian flag was a kind of sidewise blue cross on a red background with white outlining the edges of the blue cross.

"Red, white, and blue," said Jack. "Funny how

many flags are red, white, and blue, like ours." Bo tried to count the flags on the page that were red, white, and blue, but she lost count. There were lots.

"If they asked me to make a flag, I'd use a lot more colors than this," she said. "And different designs, not just stripes and stars. Too many stars. These flags are not very interesting. But I like this one with green leafs on it."

"That's Canada's flag," said Jack. "Philipe is from Canada."

"Oh," said Bo. "I will tell him I like his flag."

"He'll be very pleased," said Jack.

He put the last white frosting line on the blue cross, and when he'd finished, Bo thought it was the most beautiful cake Jack had ever made.

Then Bo and Jack cleaned up the kitchen, and Arvid came in from the blacksmith shop. They all took turns at the basin to wash their faces and hands. Arvid had to take a long time scrubbing his hands with the scrub brush because he worked with coal and lots of other dirty things. It didn't do much good—Arvid's hands never came clean.

Jack and Arvid didn't dress up. Arvid just changed into his clean work shirt. Jack didn't need a clean shirt, since his shirt had been covered with an apron. But he put on his red suspenders because Bo liked them so much.

Jack brushed out Bo's tangled braids and braided new neat ones. He put a green ribbon on the end of each braid to match her dress, which was green calico printed with red apples. Yovela had made it for her last year. Bo showed Arvid that it was getting pretty short.

Arvid said, "Yovela always gives you plenty hem. I'll just let this down next time I get a chance."

At last they were ready. They walked across the bridge, Jack carefully carrying the cake in front of him. Jack liked his cakes to be a surprise so he had put it in a box and covered it with a clean cloth. That way no one could see it.

Almost everyone was there before them—all the children and most of the grown-ups, except a few men who were hunting. Jack put the cake on the table where Milo had trays of coffee cups set out and mason jars full of forks.

When it was time, Milo called everyone to gather round. Jack took the cake out of the box while Milo pretended to be a trumpet making an important sound: *ta-ta-tatata-ta-ta!*

"By golly," Ollie said. That's what he always said—by golly. The boys called him By-Golly-Ollie to tease him.

Ollie's face was red from the home brew he'd been drinking, and it got still redder when he looked at the cake.

"By golly," he said again. "The flag."

Everyone clapped and cheered for Ollie, and Lester began singing, "For He's a Jolly Good Fellow," which was another one of Bo's favorite songs.

Before they'd even cut the cake, the door burst open and in came Clarence, red-faced and panting. Clarence was the old-timer who worked the wireless.

He was waving a piece of paper over his head. A wire.

Everyone stood frozen in place to hear what Clarence's news was. Their anxious faces made Bo suddenly afraid.

But that anxiety only lasted a second. They could tell that it wasn't bad news from the way Clarence was acting. He was so excited he was dancing up and down on his toes.

"Wait till you hear this! Airplane coming! Coming here!"

Everyone crowded around Clarence. Milo grabbed the wire from him and read it out loud once, and then again, as if he could hardly believe it. "Will Danfer flying his AJ-1 and Ted Smith, mechanic, coming from Nome to Ballard Creek, landing on the sandbar in front of town. An airplane," Milo said softly. "At Ballard Creek."

"Best surprise *I* ever had for a birthday," said Ollie.

Oscar and Bo hung on to each other, hardly breathing. Nothing so exciting had happened in Ballard Creek before.

It would be there in about a week. They'd wire ahead so that everyone would know when it was coming. The plane would make three stops, Candle and Bettles first. And then Ballard Creek.

No one in Ballard Creek had ever seen an airplane except for Cannibal Ivan. When everyone had quieted a little, they ate Ollie's cake and drank coffee while Cannibal told them all about the time he'd seen one in Fairbanks, the first airplane ever in Alaska.

"See, they was flying around, these promoters, doing flying exhibitions anyplace they could—1913 it was. Wanted to make a lot of money, big hoorah with posters all over. Charged money for people to watch the plane take off and land at the ball field. But nobody sitting on the bleachers except the fat cats and women in their big hats. Everyone else got to see it free, because how smart did you have to be to figure out that if you climbed a tree by the ballpark or sat on someone's roof, you wouldn't have to pay anything at all?"

Everyone laughed at the disgusted look on Cannibal's face. "Tomfool people, those promoters."

He showed with his hands what the plane had done.

"It took off and landed about a dozen times, tipping and turning up in the air, and the last time, the pilot threw out some balloons. They expected to sell that plane to someone, but no one was offering. So a few days later, they took it apart and shipped it on a stern-wheeler to the mouth of the Yukon and back to the States. I was on that steamer, the *Molly B*, saw the plane all wrapped up on the deck. Looked real little without its wings."

The whole country had been airplane crazy for years. Before Bo was born, some soldiers had flown from New York with four airplanes. They'd landed on a sandbar in the Yukon, and then they'd gone to

Nome. Since then, the children in Ballard Creek had been playing airplanes with old boxes and slabs of logs from the sawmill.

Now there were eighteen planes in Alaska, and all the men in Ballard Creek knew everything about those eighteen—their numbers and who owned them and everything that had happened to those planes.

And now Will Danfer's AJ-1 was coming to Ballard Creek.

Lots of young pilots were going to villages around Alaska because they wanted to show how useful planes could be. They could carry the mail and fly people to places in an hour that would take days and weeks the old ways. Maybe save lives.

It was the most useful invention that was ever invented.

Waiting for the plane was going to be worse than waiting for Christmas or the Fourth of July.

CHAPTER NINE

THE AIRPLANE

NOW NO ONE in Ballard Creek or at the mine could talk of anything else but airplanes.

All the miners who lived out on the trail past the mine walked into town through the slush and mud, and they filled up the roadhouse. No one knew when the airplane would come, but no one was going to miss it. They'd stay as long as it took.

Clarence hardly ever left the wireless cabin, waiting to hear when the plane would come, and there was always someone crowded into the little shack with him. Two days, four days, five days, six days, seven days. It was a terribly long time to wait.

Cannibal and Nels Niemi from the creeks were in the wireless shack playing checkers with Clarence when the wire came. Nels and Cannibal ran out into the street, whooping and carrying on. They didn't even wait for Clarence to print it out.

Everyone who was in town came running to hear what the wire said: "Leaving Bettles at 3:45. Ballard Creek at 4:30."

Cannibal saw Bo and shouted, "Go tell the boys! Go tell the boys!" Bo threw a troubled look at Oscar. She wanted to go tell the boys, of course—she didn't want them to miss it—but she was afraid that the plane would come while she was telling them. But then she turned and ran as fast as she could across the bridge to the mining camp.

Bo ran so hard the bottom of her feet hurt from pounding on the ground. As soon as she yelled the news to Jack, she ran back across the bridge.

Everyone in town was crowded down by the sandbar where the plane would land.

Bo pushed through the grown-ups to get to

the edge of the bank with Oscar and the other children. The children held hands and braced their feet
to keep from being pushed into the water by the
crowd behind them.

"Quiet! Quiet!" the grown-ups kept telling everyone. It had to be quiet so they could listen for the
plane.

Bo was looking at the sky so hard, she felt as if
her eyes were bruised. It seemed like a very long time
before they saw something way down the river, high
in the sky.

"Looks like a dragonfly," said Oscar. The dragonfly got bigger and bigger and then it looked like
a small bird and then like a raven and then they
could hear it. That made it real, that little sound.

"Oh, oh, oh," said Bo, and clutched Oscar's hand.
It sounded like the engine on the
winch at the mine. Or maybe

more like Arvid's sewing machine.

It got closer and closer, and then they could see the four wings and they could see two heads inside the plane, one in front and one in back.

And then it was right over their heads, flying low over the town up toward the roadhouse. Everyone left the riverbank to follow it, never taking their eyes off it for a minute. Bo's throat was sore from screeching. She tripped and fell because she wasn't watching where she was going.

The plane tipped sideways and made a circle around the roadhouse, and everyone followed it around and around, stumbling and falling in the cold mud left from the melting snow.

Everyone ran. Even all the old men and old women were running as if they were young again. They ran, heads up, craning their necks, following the plane as if it had strings and was pulling them. To the back of the roadhouse and then back to the front again the plane circled, with everyone following.

Bo fell again, and this time, strong hands reached for her and swung her up. It was Arvid. He didn't take his eyes off the plane or stop running. He just set Bo all muddy and wet on his shoulders, the way he used to when she was little.

"Gonna be trampled," was all he said. The roaring, rackety airplane suddenly came down lower, right toward the roadhouse, and everyone screamed, terrified. It was going to knock the roadhouse down! Then it missed the roadhouse—it was coming right at them!

Arvid was swearing fiercely in Swedish. From Arvid's shoulders, Bo saw old Nakuchluk standing stock-still in the path, her mouth open, but Bo couldn't hear her screaming over the sound of the plane engine.

The plane circled around once again, suddenly dipped a little to one side, and there it was, landed on the sandbar.

It happened so quickly that all the people around the roadhouse had to run back down to the bank.

Bo held her breath until the propeller in the front of the airplane stopped spinning. Then the dreadful noise stopped.

The two men in the plane climbed over the side. Bo shrank down on Arvid's shoulders, frightened because they didn't look like real people. The fliers had huge black eyes like dragon-flies, but then they pulled the eyes off their faces and let them dangle around their necks.

"Like snow goggles," Arvid told Bo. "Keeps the wind out of their eyes."

The fliers were laughing and waving at everyone. Bo was sure they'd had a good time scaring everyone, watching them scream and run. They looked pleased with themselves, like Sammy or the other big kids did when they jumped out at the little kids and scared them.

Two of the old-timers—Jimmy the Pirate and Sol—waded through the water to get to the sandbar and were shaking the pilots' hands so hard Bo thought it looked like they were pumping water.

Bo looked for Jack. She was suddenly afraid he'd missed the airplane, missed it all.

The pilot and the other man waded to the bank, shaking hands all the way, and there were Lester and all the other men from the mine, crowding around as well. But she didn't see Jack anywhere.

Then she saw him, tall as a tree, standing by the roadhouse. Nakuchluk and her old husband, Unakserak, were hiding, peeking out from behind him.

"Papa," she screamed. "Did you see it? Did you see it?"

Jack waved to her. He put his arms around Nakuchluk's and Unakserak's shoulders and encouraged them along with him to the riverbank. They still looked scared. Jack looked up at Bo on Arvid's shoulders.

"I was wondering where you was in all the hoorah," Jack said. "Wonder you kids wasn't run over, with all the carrying on."

The fliers couldn't stay long; they had to get right back to Nome while the weather was good. So after coffee and sandwiches at the roadhouse, they took off again.

They dragged the airplane down to the end of the sandbar, and then they started the noisy engine, climbed in, and pulled their goggles back over their eyes.

And there it was, the black plane hurtling down the sandbar—*rackety, rackety*. They all watched and listened while it turned into a bird again, and then a dragonfly and then they couldn't hear it anymore.

That night there was a dance and a big party, noisier than the Fourth of July, more joyful than Christmas.

It seemed to Bo that no one in Ballard Creek would ever be able to go back to their ordinary life again.

CHAPTER TEN
SLUICING AND CLEANUP

IN JUNE, WILD ROSES and bluebells crowded together under the birch trees lining the banks of the creek. Bluebells and roses always grew together, as if they were best friends, Bo thought. And as if they knew how pretty they looked together, pink and blue.

The first mosquitoes were gone, the lazy, slow-moving, long-legged ones that hid all winter under the spruce bark. Now the summer mosquitoes had hatched, much smaller and more ornery. Some years the mosquitoes weren't so bad. Not this year, though.

Mosquitoes were everywhere Bo looked, and swarms of them rose up in the air when she ran through the tall grass. Their thin, tinny whining against the mosquito screen by Bo's bed was so loud that sometimes she had to close her ears with her fingers before she could fall asleep.

Jack kept a smudgepot smoldering outside the cookshack door to keep the mosquitoes out, but still they got in through the thin smoke and fell into the oatmeal and got baked into the cookies.

Mosquito time was cleanup time. Cleanup was when the miners found out how much gold they had in the pay dirt they'd been piling up all winter.

They had to shovel all that pay dirt into the long wooden sluice boxes and wash it to get the gold out. The boxes were called sluice boxes because *sluicing* meant "washing," Arvid told her.

And it was called pay dirt because when all the gold was taken out of it, they could sell the gold and get paid.

Bo nodded her head to show she understood all that. "But what I don't see is where the gold comes from," she said.

"Better ask Peter," said Arvid. "He'll explain it better than me."

So when Peter was leaving the cookshack after breakfast, Bo pulled his sleeve. "About the gold," she said. "How did it get into the pay dirt?"

"Now, that's an amazing thing," Peter said, smiling. He liked to explain about rocks to Bo.

Peter sat down next to her on the bench at the long table and peered earnestly into her face, like he always did when he was explaining something.

"Millions and millions of years ago," he said, "the gold in our pay dirt formed in some rocks. Happens all the time. Different rocks, different things form in them when they cool down or get squeezed. Like that mica you see shining in rocks. And those little red garnets I showed you in the schist, that stripey rock."

Bo nodded to show she was listening hard.

"Now remember I told you how rocks change? All the mountains that ever were get turned into sand someday."

"I remember," said Bo. "But it never seems true."

"I know," said Peter. "People just can't imagine it. Hard for me, too." He lit his pipe and puffed on it to make a little flame spurt up.

"Well, for millions of years, those rocks with gold in them were parts of a mountain. And those mountains were getting worn down to boulders and rocks. And the rocks with gold in them got tumbled down the creeks, down the rivers. Got all smashed and pounded into gravel and sand. You know gold is very heavy—heavier than water, heavier than gravel and sand," Peter said. "So the gold that was in the sand and gravel sank straight down to the bottom of the creeks and rivers. Then after more millions of years, the creeks were buried and buried again. And again.

"Now, the gold's deep down in the gravel and dirt in the cracks of the bedrock. Underground. It couldn't go any deeper because the bedrock is like a solid floor underground, not broken into bits like rocks on the top of the earth." Peter leaned back and put his hands on his thighs.

"And that's why we dug the shaft down to bedrock. That's where the gold ended up after all those millions of years. Bedrock's where we have to dig the pay dirt out."

ALL WINTER long, the boys had been underground in the cold dark. They had carbide lamps on their

hats, and their pockets were full of candles that they'd put in the holders in the walls of the tunnels.

But still it was dark down there.

Before they could dig out any pay dirt, they had to thaw the frozen ground with steam. The steam came from the boiler through long rubber pipes to the steam probes. One man would hold the probe while the other hammered it into the ground.

They'd leave the probes overnight, and in the morning, they would shovel the thawed ground, which had turned to boiling hot muck, into their wheelbarrows.

They'd push the wheelbarrows to the square bucket that was sitting at the bottom of the shaft. It was a big bucket, and it could hold three wheel-barrow loads. Sometimes the bucket had to carry a man up to the top, like last year when Alex had taken sick down there and couldn't go up the ladder.

Then the steam winch hauled the bucket up out of the shaft and took it zinging along the cable across the diggings to the gin pole, and the bucket tripped there so that the load would dump on the pile of pay dirt.

Bo was not allowed near the diggings when the winch was working. Everyone had seen what could happen when the cable snapped. Phillipe had two fingers missing that a cable had whipped off.

She wasn't allowed in the boiler house, either. That was where Dan kept the big fire roaring and snapping under the boiler. He fed that fire with cords and cords of wood. And he had to keep the boiler filled with water, too. Bo thought Danny had the hardest job of all.

When they weren't using the steam for the probes, the boiler made steam for the winch and the buzz saw.

Boilers were dangerous. The boys all knew stories about boilers blowing up, sending scalding steam and pieces of the red-hot iron over everyone.

There were a lot of bad accidents at mining camps.

After the snow was almost gone, the boys

couldn't go underground anymore. It wasn't safe. In the winter, the ground around the shaft stayed frozen, and the sides of the tunnels were frozen. But in the summer the sides of the tunnels might begin to slough off. And sometimes there was too much bad gas underground when the weather got warm.

So they'd stopped digging and had started all the work that must be done before sluicing. They'd been getting ready for weeks, stacking up cords and cords of wood by the boiler house to run the steam pump and the winches and the buzz saw.

They'd repaired the sluice boxes and made new ones with boards they sawed at the saw pit.

The sluice boxes had to be perfectly smooth inside so that no gold would catch on the splinters. Bo sat with Johnny and Karl while they planed and sanded those boards. They gave her all the curls of yellow wood to play with.

"Feel that," Karl said, showing her the board he'd finished. "Smooth as a baby's bottom!" Bo didn't know what a baby's bottom would feel like, but the board *was* smooth. Just like the satin band on her favorite blanket.

"The boards have to fit together perfectly so

there won't be any cracks for the tiny bits of gold to
hide in," Johnny said. So Johnny and Karl fitted and
sanded and planed and fitted some more until there
wasn't even a tiny space between the boards to trap
flakes of gold.

Then the boys put together all the sluice boxes
so that they made one long wooden trough slanting

down from the pile of pay dirt to the bank of the creek. The pump was tested and primed, the canvas hose was checked for holes, and at last they were ready.

Now they needed water to wash the gold out of the pay dirt. The water in Ballard Creek was low and sluggish after the long winter, and if there was not enough water, there would be no sluicing, and there would be no gold. Not enough water was the worst thing that could happen to a mining camp.

But in a few days, the snow in the hills melted, and the nearly empty creek was suddenly filled with rushing, icy water. It tumbled the rocks on the bottom of the creek, making a lovely clattery sound. Bo wanted to wade into that rushing creek and feel the water pull hard at her boots.

When Arvid saw her staring at the creek from the cookshack window, he knew what she was thinking. He scowled fiercely at Bo. "You stay out of there. No playing in the creek when it's this high and this fast."

"I wouldn't," Bo said in an insulted way, as if she'd never thought of such a thing.

THE BOYS quickly made a dam for the creek so the water would fill the sluicing pond, and they were ready to go. The pump would be sunk into the sluicing pond, and the big hose would be attached to the pump. When they turned the pump on, the powerful surge of water from the hose would wash the pay dirt down the sluice boxes.

At lunchtime, the boss said, "Tomorrow we'll start double shifts." That meant some of the men would work in the day, and when they were finished, the rest of the boys would work all night. Bo remembered double shifts last year, when she'd had to be extra quiet all day because some of the boys were in the bunkhouse sleeping.

Now that there was water for sluicing, everyone had to work very, very fast without stopping, around the clock, because you never knew when the water would dry up.

Even Jack would leave the kitchen and work at sluicing. The boss couldn't waste a big, strong man like Jack in the kitchen when it was cleanup time.

But Bo didn't really like it when things were so

mixed up and the papas weren't where they were supposed to be.

GITNOO CAME EARLY to cook the breakfast in Jack's place. She shook Bo awake, which she'd never done before. Bo sat up in bed and stared at Gitnoo.

"Tell everyone grizzly tracks down by the spring," Gitnoo told Bo. Bo knew why Gitnoo was excited. A grizzly was not something you wanted to have hanging around.

Jack had been on the porch, washing up. He came inside, toweling his hair, his eyebrows raised in a question. "What's Gitnoo all bothered about?"

Gitnoo made a bear's toe-in walk with her hands to show Jack.

"Grizzly tracks," Bo said. "Down by the spring."

"Hmm," Jack said. "Good thing you're staying home today to help with sluicing." He took the rifle down from its peg over the door and checked to see that it was loaded. Then he hung it back up and said, "Probably that bear's just moving cross-country, but we'll keep our eyes open."

"I'm going to sleep now," Jack told her. "In the bunkhouse. I can't sleep in here worrying about what Gitnoo is doing." Jack stretched, his huge arms about bursting his shirtsleeves. "Help Gitnoo all you can." He bent to kiss the top of her head and went out the door.

Jack had mixed the batter for the hotcakes the night before, so the boys had a good breakfast, though they didn't like the way Gitnoo fried their hotcakes. She left them on the griddle too long, so they got tough.

"Shoe leathers," the boys called the hotcakes Gitnoo made. Bo didn't like them that way either, but as long as you could put syrup on them, you could eat them. There were no biscuits or bacon or sausage, but there was oatmeal. Not a breakfast that Jack would have given them, but they didn't complain. They just teased Gitnoo as usual and pulled Bo's braids when they left.

The boys were interested in what Gitnoo had to say about the grizzly. No chance that any bear would come near the diggings with the noise from the pump and boiler and all, but they warned Bo about going near the spring.

CHAPTER ELEVEN

NOT ENOUGH

IT WAS VERY HOT the first day of sluicing, but the boys couldn't take off their heavy shirts or their hot leather gloves because of the mosquitoes. Most of the boys even wore their long underwear all summer for protection from the mosquitoes. The keening mosquitoes would cover their shirts and pants, but their stingers couldn't reach skin through the layers of wool.

The only way they could protect their faces was with a head-net and hat, but the boys were like Bo and didn't like to look through the net. Except Guillaume. He wore his head-net all day.

"I can't stand them pests. Drives me crazy," he said when they teased him. "What I really can't stand," he said, "is when they brush against my lips. I hate that feeling."

Bo knew just what Guillaume meant. She hated that feeling too.

Arvid and Jack slathered citronella on Bo, every place her skin showed, but still she was bitten. The worst bites were over a bony place like her elbow or shins, or on her fingers. Bo scratched her mosquito bites until they bled, and that made them stop itching a little.

Some of the boys rubbed mud on their faces when the mosquitoes were really mean, like right after a rain, and they tried lots of other things. Philipe and Fritz used bacon grease on their faces. They said the mosquitoes didn't like to get their feet in it.

But because they were wearing their shirts and woolen underwear and their hot, hot rubber boots, their faces were running sweat, and so the mud and bacon grease didn't last very long when they were sluicing.

BO'S JOB was to bring the boys water. One of them pumped water from the creek to fill a barrel near the sluice boxes. Then Bo stood on a sawed-off log to fill her bucket half full. She could really carry more, but if the bucket was full, somehow she always sloshed it out on the way to the boys.

It was very noisy at the sluice boxes. The pump in the pond loudly sucked the water up through the canvas hose, and the water shooting from the hose made a great racket. So nobody tried to talk, they just made talking faces and used their hands to explain things.

Lester and Johnny were working at the first sluice box, shoveling the pay dirt into it very fast. Little Paddy stood at the front of the box, clutching the big canvas hose swollen fat with the water from the pond, guiding the nozzle. The churning water flowed down the sluice boxes, carrying off the light dirt and gravel, and the heavy gold sank right away to the bottom of the sluice boxes, where it was trapped by the riffles. Riffles were iron bars that slowed

the water down enough so that the gold would sink and not be swept away.

Arvid and Sandor and Andy were working the rest of the row of sluice boxes, snatching out all the big rocks that had been in the pay dirt. Rocks would block the flow of water, and gold could be lost if the water was spilling over the sides of the sluice box.

Bo brought her first bucket to Lester. He dropped his shovel, grinned at her, and grabbed up the bucket. He drank deeply, his head thrown back, picked up his shovel and went back to work again.

Then Bo trotted back to the barrel to get water for Johnny, and she went back and forth like that all morning, down one side of the sluice box and then up the other, then back to where Guillaume in his head-net and Fritz were tending to the hose.

Some of the boys drank the bucket dry. And the ones who didn't poured the rest over themselves to cool off.

Bo's arms were sore from straining to keep the bucket from banging into her leg, her hands were numb from the icy creek water in the barrel, and she hated it when the water sloshed onto her overall legs. But she was proud to do her job.

The rocks and gravel they threw out of the sluice boxes were called tailings. The tailing piles were what was left over after the sluicing was done. There were tailing piles all around the mining camp. They were very good places to play, because you could find interesting rocks. And it was always nice to be up higher than everyone else.

But there were special spiders that lived in the tailing piles, really, really big spiders. When she was little, Bo used to scream every time she saw one. But Arvid said she was silly. The spiders liked little girls and just wanted to play. Bo could see that was true, but she still wasn't so sure she liked them very much. She always got up and moved away when one came to play with her.

Jack had told Bo she had to go back to the cook-shack to help Gitnoo when it was almost noon. But Bo was not to ring the triangle at lunchtime because eight of the men were sleeping in the bunkhouse and it might wake them up.

The boys didn't come to eat all at once, but two at a time. Lester and Johnny were first. They didn't bother to wash their sweaty faces or dirty hands, and they ate fast, hardly saying a word, because two more were waiting their turn to eat. Gitnoo had the big platter stacked high with caribou sandwiches, and Bo brought them each a bowl of the potato salad Jack had made last night.

Gitnoo poured their coffee and put a huge piece of chocolate cake on each plate, and when they'd finished, they stood up, grabbed another sandwich, smiled at Bo and Gitnoo, and left in a rush. In just a few minutes, Fritz and Andy came banging into the cookshack and ate just as fast as Lester and Johnny had.

When all the boys on the day shift had eaten and Bo was helping Gitnoo with the dishes, there was a sudden silence. The pump had stopped.

"Time to clean out the box," Gitnoo said.

Every few hours, the boys would stop shoveling pay dirt. They'd shut the water off and then they'd take up the riffles. Carefully they'd sweep all the gold and sand out of the sluice boxes into a gold pan, and carefully they'd wash the riffles. They'd clean all the cracks with a little brush, ever so slowly, ever so thoroughly. Every bit of gold had to be removed. It was very painstaking, finicky work, but they'd do it many times until all the pay dirt had been sluiced.

Bo and Gitnoo went to watch them for a while, but it wasn't really very interesting, so they didn't stay long.

In two days, they'd sluiced all the pay dirt, and after they'd all had a good night's sleep, it was time to finish cleaning the gold.

After breakfast, Arvid brought one of Gitnoo's small washtubs into the cookshack and set it on the table. Bo climbed on the bench and looked into the tub. The gold was dirty, mixed with black sand and fine gravel. And it didn't even fill half the tub.

Here was all the gold they'd cleaned out of the sluice boxes so very carefully. Here was all the gold they'd dug in the long winter. That big mountain of pay dirt had been hiding just half a washtub of gold.

NOW THEY MUST clean the gold again, so thoroughly that there was no dirt or sand in with it at all. Jack brought in the big galvanized tub, which Jack used for Bo's bath, and Bo helped him fill it with water from the rain barrel.

They must first pan the gold to wash away all the sand and dirt. Sandor and Peter were the best at panning, and they weren't at all modest about being the best. "This here is an art," Sandor told Bo. "Takes years to learn the right technique."

Gold pans were shallow, with sloping sides and a flat bottom. They came in all sizes, and there were dozens of them around the mine. They were very useful. Bo used one for all her crayons, and Jack used the biggest one for putting sliced bread or maybe cinnamon buns on the table. And the boys used one out on the porch for shaving.

But today they'd use the gold pans for gold. Sandor and Peter filled their pans with some of the dirty gold from the washtub. Then, quickly and skillfully, they twisted and swirled the pans in the water so that the sand and dirt floated away and the gold stayed at the bottom of the pan.

Sandor filled a pan and held it out to Bo. "Try it." Bo had been wishing she could, but the pan was so big and heavy when it was filled that she couldn't make circles with it the way Sandor and Peter did.

Sandor came behind her and held her hands on the pan, and together they washed all the little pebbles and dirt away. There at the bottom of the pan were nuggets of gold, glowing clean and beautiful in the sunlight slanting through the cookshack windows.

When Sandor and Peter finished the panning, they put all the clean gold in a dishpan. Then they put the dishpan on the warm stove so the gold would dry.

All of this took a long time. The boys who were working outside, taking apart the sluice boxes and putting away the canvas hoses, came in from time to time to look at the gold and eat and smoke a pipe. Jack had sandwiches and soup and a big caribou roast and four pies and three cakes laid out on the table for anyone who was hungry. They'd be in and out of the cookshack all day, not eating regular meals, until the job was all finished.

When the gold in the dish pan was dry, the boss and Arvid and Peter put the gold through screens to sort it into different sizes. Bo liked the biggest nuggets the best, because they were funny shapes and all different. She crowded between Pete and Arvid to see all the big ones.

"Look!" Bo pointed to a long, flattish nugget. "That one looks like a weasel!" Arvid raised his eyebrows at Peter and laughed. Jack stopped wiping the stew pan and bent over Bo to look.

"See?" she told him. "You know how they run, all humpety. It looks like a weasel running."

Jack nodded. "I believe it does," he said, and Bo smiled up at him.

"Just think," said Peter, "how long it took to make those nuggets, how many millions of years. And now they're up here on top of the earth, all cleaned up and shining. Makes you think, doesn't it?"

The finest gold was the hardest to clean. The boss put it in a special copper pan and passed a magnet over it to pull out the black sand. Black sand, Peter told Bo, was ground down from magnetic rocks. When he had finished with the magnet, Peter shook the pan and blew on the gold to get the finest sand off, the sand that wasn't magnetic.

And that was the end of cleanup.

All the piles of nuggets were carefully weighed on the little gold scale. Then they were packed into little canvas bags, each size in a different bag. The gold dust and even the black sand were packed up too. The boss would take it all to Fairbanks to sell and then the boys would get their pay for the year.

BO COULD SEE that the boys were disappointed, because they weren't talking and joking as much as usual.

She asked Arvid about it when he was tucking her into bed. "Wasn't there enough?"

"Could have been better," he said. "Got to make some more tunnels, come fall, different direction." He pulled her blanket up under her chin.

"That's mining," he said. "Work the ground till you run out of ground, no more gold. Close up and go somewhere else."

"Well, we'll never have to go somewhere else, will we?"

Arvid stood up and turned to leave.

"Gold don't last forever," he said.

CHAPTER TWELVE
VISITING OLAF

THE MIDDLE of the summer was a good time to be outdoors because it was nesting time for the hundreds of birds who'd come north in the spring. Bo hardly ever saw them, but they sang in the deep woods all day long.

"Never heard such a loud bunch of birds," Jack used to say.

One morning in July, Bo asked the papas if she could visit Olaf. Olaf was one of the miners who lived out on the creeks north of Ballard Creek. Bo liked to visit Olaf because of his "children." That's what he called his pets. He had a ptarmigan, a wea-sel, a porcupine, a dog, and a raven. They all lived together happily and didn't have fights. Bo always tried to get there at noon so she could help feed them.

"Well, sure," Arvid said. "If you can get someone to go with you."

Bo had to have a grown-up with her when she visited Olaf, because he lived two miles away and there might be bears or moose on the trail. So she had to go with someone who had a gun.

"No one's seen any sign of that grizzly," Arvid said. "No one's seen any black bears, for that matter. Probably all of them up in the hills looking for early berries.

"Still," he said. "Can't go that far without a gun." He thought for a minute. "Who could go with you? Town's nearly cleared out," he said. That was true. So many people were gone in the summer—the men and boys hunting caribou, the women and children down the river at fish camp.

"Big Annie didn't go anywhere," said Bo. Big Annie was all alone because Charlie Sickik, her hus-band, was hunting caribou and the twins were gone.

"Well, ask her, then," said Jack.

Arvid nodded. "Big Annie's a good one." He said that because Big Annie was a good shot with her .30-06. Sometimes on the Fourth of July, they'd have a shooting contest with targets. Big Annie always had her shot in the black center.

Bo ran across the bridge to ask Annie, and Annie said she'd be glad to go with Bo—just give her half an hour, and she'd be ready.

"I'll wrap up some bread for Olaf," Jack said when Bo came back.

Big Annie wasn't really big at all, but everyone called her that because one of her twins was named Annie. So everyone called them Big Annie and Little Annie. Betty was the other twin. They were eleven. Bo knew that twins were supposed to look alike, but Little Annie and Betty didn't look a bit alike.

The twins had gone with their grandmother Nakuchluk to visit in Kotzebue. All the Eskimos in Ballard Creek had relatives in Kotzebue. Every year they'd go there to get some seal or whale oil, which they couldn't get in Ballard Creek because seals and whales lived in the ocean, and Ballard Creek was far away from the ocean.

Seal oil was the Eskimos' favorite food, and they put it on everything they ate: dried fish and caribou roasts and even blueberries. Almost everyone loved seal oil. But Bo didn't, and Oscar didn't either. He said it made him want to throw up.

Big Annie and Bo walked along the trail to Preacher Creek, holding hands, both happy to be outdoors on such a beautiful day. As they walked along the trail, Bo would stop every now and again to listen to the trees. If you put your ear up to the trunk of a birch or aspen, you could hear the tree talking when it bent a little in the wind. Sometimes it sounded as if the tree was singing, and it was a different song every day.

The streaks of sap running down the trunks of the spruce trees were soft, because it had been so hot. Big Annie stopped to peel some off to chew. She gave some to Bo, and Bo chewed it, but she made a face. Spruce pitch didn't taste very good. It never did. Bo couldn't see why Eskimos liked to chew spruce sap. But she kept trying it, hoping that it would taste better next time.

OLAF WAS HAPPY to see them, and so were the animals. First the raven hopped over and pecked at the beads on Bo's moccasins. He had many colors in his glossy black feathers—blue and green and gold. He shimmered with colors.

Dog pushed his head into their hands for a pet, wagged his thick, shaggy tail in slow circles, smiling with his kind eyes. Dog was raggedy, shedding his winter coat in big tufts that floated in the sunlight and caught on the rough boards of his doghouse.

Dog couldn't see very well, and he couldn't really hear at all.

"He don't go far, now he can't see good, but I worry about bears. Don't think he can smell, either," Olaf said in a sad way. "He wouldn't know if a bear was walking by his side."

Bo walked around the yard, saying hello to each one of the animals.

"Can we feed them now?"

"In a bit," Olaf said, laughing at her. "Come inside and rest a minute."

He took them inside his cabin and poured Big Annie a cup of coffee from the pot on the back of the stove.

"You tell Jack I thank him for this bread," he said. "Nobody makes bread like Jack." Olaf made his own bread, too, of course, but Bo knew it was true about Jack's bread.

There was a picture of Olaf's sister Birgit on the wall over the table. She still lived in Germany, where Olaf came from. Olaf said his sister was a little older now, same as him. Birgit was so pretty. She had her braids in a circle on top of her head like Arvid's mother in the picture Arvid had. Bo knelt on the chair and reached up to touch her face. "Birgit," she said. It always felt as if she was visiting Birgit, too.

A suit of clean clothes—pants and jacket—hung on a nail. All the miners kept a suit of good clothes ready, in case something came up that they couldn't wear their filthy mining clothes to. Going-to-town clothes they called them.

There were two moosehide bags on the table. Olaf had finished his cleanup, and the next time he was in Ballard, he'd send his gold out to the mint with the scowman.

"Got something to show you," he said. He picked up one bag and poured the nuggets into a brass pan with a narrow end. He sorted through the nuggets with his scarred finger until he found the one he was looking for.

"Look at this one," he said. "Looks just like a bird." And it did. It was perfectly shaped like a flying bird with its wings spread out. Bo pulled in her breath and touched the nugget bird with one finger. Big Annie bent over the little nugget and touched it too.

"*Pinnaknaktuk*," she said. Pretty.

Olaf put the bird nugget into a white envelope, and he wrote on it with a little stub of a pencil. He showed Bo that he'd written her name on the envelope.

"I'll give your papas this one to make a little ring for you," he said. Bo was too pleased to say anything. She just looked at Olaf with shining eyes. He picked out another nugget, a sort of squashed circle shape, and he handed that to Big Annie. "This one's for you," he said. Big Annie beamed at Olaf.

There never was much gold on Olaf's claim, but Olaf was sure that he would sometime find a big fat streak of gold and he'd be rich.

But he hadn't found it last winter.

"It don't bother me," he said. "I'm happy with the little bit I found, enough to buy my grubstake for the winter, maybe a new pair of boots."

All the men out on the creeks did their mining by hand. They didn't have the boiler house or the steam winch or the buzz saw or the steam pump like they had at the Ballard Creek mine. They just had a swede saw, a pick and shovel, an ax, and a winch they wound up by hand.

They dug their shafts by thawing the frozen ground with a fire. When the fire burned out, they moved the charred wood aside and dug out the thawed dirt. Then they made another fire, in the hole, and they kept doing this until they reached bedrock.

Olaf said he could dig one foot in one day. It had taken him twelve days to dig his shaft, so he knew it was twelve feet deep.

"Two years ago Sven Anderson down by Bettles—" Olaf broke off to say to Annie, "You remember Sven," and Annie nodded. "Sven dug all the way to bedrock one fall, but in the spring ground-water flooded in and filled up the shaft." Olaf shook his head and poured himself some coffee. "All that work for nothing," said Olaf. "But that's the mining life. It's still a good way to earn a living. Don't hurt no one, don't rob no one, just take the gold clean from nature."

Bo didn't know anything about earning a living any other way, but Big Annie did.

"Too much work, mining," she said. "Better live like an Eskimo."

CHAPTER THIRTEEN

OLAF'S FAMILY

BIG ANNIE HAD never seen Olaf's family, so while he puttered around the kitchen, Olaf told her how he got them all.

First Olaf had Dog and then, a few years ago, Dog had sniffed out a whole batch of fluffy ptarmigan babies hiding in the tall grass by the trail. No mother or father anywhere.

The babies had followed him right from the beginning. Some of them had flown away in the fall, but most of them came back from time to time to eat at the feedpan. At least Olaf thought they were his ptarmigan.

"Maybe just a bunch of freeloaders," Olaf said. "But Harvey, he never went anywhere. Been with me since he was a baby."

Olaf said he wasn't even sure Harvey could fly. He just followed Olaf around, his little fat body waddling, making his crazy ratcheting sounds as he walked around the yard.

Bo thought ptarmigans were the most beautiful birds that ever were in the winter, with their velvety white roundness and that little bit of black on the tail when they flew. But in the summer, ptarmigan feathers turned red-brown and black and scragglylooking from molting. Even the feathers on their feet changed colors in the summer.

The raven was named Shine. "That's the best name for him," Bo explained to Big Annie, "because look how ravens are, like they are oiled and polished, like Jack does my boots. All the black feathers shine and their long beaks, too. Even their eyes are shiny!"

Bo thought a minute. "How *do* ravens get shiny like that?"

But Olaf didn't know.

Olaf had found Shine with his wing torn half off. "Maybe a fox, maybe a hawk hurt him," Olaf said. He didn't know how old Shine was, but he thought he must be young because he had healed so easily. Olaf put ointment on what was left of the torn wing, and it healed into a sort of wing stump.

Shine couldn't fly anymore, but he could hop marvelously high, straight up. "Like he has springs in his legs," Olaf said. He'd hop on the braces for the winch, peer into the shaft, and call out to Olaf when he was down there digging.

"Ravens can nearly talk, you know," Olaf said. "They have a lot of different calls. I never counted them properly, but I figure it's about twenty different calls. This one now, Shine, he don't use all of them, because he don't have a normal raven life. Sometimes other ravens fly over, sit in the spruce trees there, and call out to him. Sometimes he answers and sometimes not."

"I like the sound they make that's like knocking on wood," said Bo. "The one that sounds like *bonk, bonk, bonk*. What does that one mean?"

"I like that one too," said Olaf. "But Shine doesn't make it, and I never figured what it means. Someday I'm going to find me a book tells all about ravens."

"Don't need a book," said Big Annie. "You ask my father. He knows all the raven calls. The old Eskimos learned them good."

Olaf looked surprised at Annie.

"Ravens talk to Unakserak," she said.

"By god, I'll *do* that," Olaf said in a thoughtful way. "I'll ask Unakserak."

Oxadak, Oscar's father, had brought the porcupine to Olaf. Oxadak had killed the porcupine's mother for supper. Porcupine was good eating, everyone said. But Oxadak didn't kill the porcupine baby. He put it in his hat and took it back to the house to show to Oscar. Oscar told his father they should take the baby to Olaf, and they did.

"Oscar's the one named him Fred," said Olaf.

The porcupine's talk was a little high whistle. He didn't open his mouth to make the sound; it came from inside his head somewhere. He waddled slowly, didn't pay much attention to the other animals, and spent a lot of time in the trees.

"The other animals, they know not to mess with a porcupine," said Olaf. "I worried about Dog some. Dogs is notorious for bothering porcupines, get their faces stuck full of quills. Terrible mess. But I guess Dog is old enough to know better."

The weasel wasn't orphaned or hurt; it just started to live under Olaf's storage shed where he kept the mining tools.

"He'd poke his head out to look at all the customers promenading in the yard, and I was worried he'd go after the ptarmigan. Thought I'd have to get rid of him. He must have been pretty young to change his ways. He started to come out and eat when they were finished, and pretty soon, he was sitting up on the winch with the raven looking down at me, and now him and Dog are best friends. I named him Calvin for the president, but to tell you the truth, I think Calvin's a girl."

Olaf stepped out the cabin door to call the animals to him. It was time for lunch.

He had a special loud whistle, two little fingers stuck in the corners of his mouth. *SCREE! SCREE!*

Bo had tried and tried to whistle like Olaf since she was small, but she still couldn't. Just a lot of air leaked out around her little fingers. Big Annie tried to make the whistle too, but she couldn't do it either. She and Bo laughed at each other.

"I whistle just with my mouth," said Annie. She did, but it was a very weak sound compared to Olaf's whistle.

"Chuck, chuck," Olaf called.

The weasel ran across the yard to Olaf, his back humpity-humping like a hurrying caterpillar. All of Olaf's other children came too, none as fast as the weasel, but all coming.

Olaf set four beat-up tin pans and one gold pan on the bench by his cabin door. He scooped dry oatmeal from a bucket into one dish. "That's for Harvey," he said. Bo set the bowl carefully in front

of the ptarmigan, who was making his best sound—like the winch engine at the mine—start-up slow, faster, faster. Harvey bent his head immediately to the dish and went to work. Peck, peck, peck.

Then Olaf gave Bo a bowl with some special crackers he'd baked from fish and oats. "Put some of those in Harvey's pan, too," he said. Bo did and then wiped her hands on her overall pants because the crackers smelled so terrible.

Olaf went in the cabin and came out with a tin plate of table scraps—left over hotcakes and last night's stew. "Put these in Dog's dish," he told her, "the gold pan. That's his dish. But save some for Shine, too. He likes scraps better than anything."

Olaf and Bo put out dried fruit and oatmeal for Fred the porcupine, boiled fish for Calvin the weasel, boiled fish and the rest of the scraps for Shine the raven. And a few fish crackers for everyone.

"Dog eats everything, and so do Shine and Calvin. They aren't fussy," Olaf said. "Fred and Harvey are the fussiest. But both of them, porcupine and ptarmigan, can get their own food around here if they don't like what I give them. The weasel, too, for that matter."

Just Shine and Dog relied on him for their food—
Dog because he was so old, and Shine because he
was crippled.

Now that they'd eaten, Dog and Calvin were
stretched out together in the warm sun, back to back.
Bo squatted down and stroked their warm fur, Dog's
all messy and tattered, the weasel's coat sleek brown,
his belly white. They both stretched a little when she
stroked them, then settled back to sleep.

Bo looked around at all the animals in the yard—
Dog and Calvin, Harvey the ptarmigan, Fred the
porcupine, and Shine the raven. When she was with
them, she felt all stuffed up with crying and laughing at the same time.

When she'd told Jack about that mixed-up feeling before, he'd said that feeling was love. "And
a damned uncomfortable feeling it is sometimes,"
he'd said.

CHAPTER FOURTEEN
BO RUNS

BIG ANNIE AND BO left Olaf when the sun was a little lower. Jack and Arvid always told her not to stay too long when she visited. Everyone had a lot of work to do in the summer.

Bo stopped to look at a grove of aspens growing together straight and tall. She liked the way the aspen leaves shimmered and danced on their stems, as if the whole tree was shaking. Birch leaves didn't do that. The aspens had pale greeny-gray bark, which was a color Bo loved. It wasn't in her crayon box, so she didn't know what that color was called.

They were halfway home when Bo practiced

skipping. She'd been trying hard to learn how, but it was impossible until Lilly told her to sing a song in her head so her feet would keep the rhythm. That worked, so she was singing "Skip to My Lou" to herself and skipping very nicely.

But after a bit, skipping—taking such little steps—made her feet feel tight, held back. She was wearing her summer moccasins, which were so light on her feet she felt she could skim along the road like a dragonfly. It was a rule not to run in the woods because bears—even dogs—would chase anything that was moving fast. It was their nature. And she was never to get ahead of the person with the gun.

But the trail was hard and dry—perfect—so she stopped skipping and started to sprint.

"You're just like a dog," Jack used to say. "Got to break out running from time to time."

Bo had just remembered that she wasn't supposed to run or get ahead of Annie. She'd almost stopped so Annie could catch up with her when she saw an orangish shape in the willows. She turned her head to see what it was and stumbled with shock.

It was the grizzly.

He had been eating something small and bloody, a rabbit maybe, and Bo had startled him. He stood up quickly to look at her with his little black eyes. Then he dropped to all fours and started after her— just loping, not full speed.

"Annie!" she screamed, and fled, terrified, though she'd heard it said a hundred times never to run from a bear. "Annie," she screamed, "Annie!"

Big Annie was right behind the bear. "BO, LIE DOWN NOW!" Annie screamed. "NOW! NOW!"

Bo did, just fell flat on the trail and hid her face in the dirt.

The minute she did, she heard Annie's gun, a huge noise right over her head. And she heard the grunt the bear made and the sound of him hitting the ground. Still she didn't lift up her head. Another shot, and then another one.

Annie was talking to herself in Eskimo as she ran up to Bo—"yaqhii, yaqhii, yaqhii"—oh my, oh my, oh my. Bo felt Annie's strong hands lift her up. "Yaqhii, yaqhii," was all Annie could say. She pushed Bo's head against her shoulder and rocked her back and forth for what seemed like a long time.

Finally, Bo lifted her head off Annie's shoulder and looked behind her. There was the bear, an orangish heap in the trail right behind her.

His face was so sweet that Bo started to cry. She hated it that he was dead, that there was a puddle of blood pooling under his soft fur.

Annie wasn't a big woman and shouldn't have been carrying a big girl like Bo, but she didn't put Bo down; she just looped her rifle on its strap over her shoulder and carried Bo all the way back to the mine.

Annie and Bo got to the cookshack just as all the boys were sitting down to lunch. As soon as they saw Big Annie's face, they knew something was wrong.

Jack put the plate of caribou down and took Bo from Annie's arms. All the boys froze in place, silent, waiting to hear what dreadful thing had happened.

"Is it Olaf?" Jack said.

Annie shook her head. She sat down on the chair Jack put out for her, and he handed her a mug of water.

Annie was so upset she forgot her English. She started to tell them in Eskimo what had happened, so they all looked at Bo to tell them what Annie was saying. Then in the middle of a sentence, Annie switched to English.

"That bear going around here, he was by the trail. Bo was running. The bear started to chase her, just slowly, long legs just stretching out." Annie showed with her hands how the bear's legs had looked taking long steps.

"I couldn't shoot, or I'd hit Bo too. So I yell for her to lie down. And she just laid down right that minute. Just falled down like she was dead. And I shot the bear before he reached her. If she didn't lie down, he would have had her. She just do what I say, and I shoot. She do what I say."

"Jesus, Annie," said Lester. He got up from his bench and came over to her. "I want to shake your hand." Sandor jumped to his feet and bent down to give Annie a hug.

Jack tightened his hold on Bo. "Annie," said Jack, but he didn't finish what he was going to say. Bo could feel a quiver all through Jack's big body.

Arvid had been swearing softly in Swedish since Annie told them about the bear, patting Bo's back with his big hand. The boys took turns coming up to Annie to shake her hand, to touch Bo's hair or squeeze her shoulder.

"You did just right, Bo. You did what Annie told you," Lester said.

"By god, I don't know if I could have done it," said Peter.

"Good girl, Bo," Karl said, patting her.

Bo felt terrible that everyone was praising her. She had done what

she'd been told never to do. She looked up into Jack's eyes.

"I was running, and I wasn't supposed to. And I just couldn't stop running. He wouldn't have chased me if I didn't run. I wish he wasn't killed." Bo hid her face in Jack's shirt and began to cry that hard kind of crying that makes your mouth square.

"Maybe he wasn't going to hurt me," Bo sobbed. "He had a nice face."

CHAPTER FIFTEEN

FOURTH OF JULY

FOURTH OF JULY was the most important time in Ballard Creek. All the miners out at the creeks came in for it, and everyone wore their best clothes for the big dinner at the roadhouse. Lilly made Bo a new dress, pale pink with a dark pink sash around the waist.

Jack looked at the dress and sighed. "I can just imagine what you're going to do to this," he said. "Roughneck like you shouldn't be wearing any girlie colors."

The boys were excited about the Fourth, especially about all the contests. They argued back and forth over the long table about who was going to win what, and they made bets with each other. There was the wood-chopping contest, arm wrestling, knife throwing, and target shooting. And of course the footraces.

Jack would be busy for days, getting ready for the Fourth.

He would make ten or fifteen pies, and after that, he'd make the doughnuts. Everyone in Ballard Creek loved doughnuts, and Jack was the only one who could make them.

Bo was busy helping Jack. First Jack made the piecrust dough. When he'd rolled out the circles of crust, Bo's job was to pick the mosquito bodies out of them. Then Jack could put the crusts in the pan and spoon in the filling. The mosquitoes were thick this summer. Jack burned Buhach powder in the cookshack to keep them down, but when they died in the smoke, they just fell straight down onto the crusts while Jack was rolling them out. It was a great nuisance.

Jack made pumpkin pies with canned pumpkin, blueberry pies with last year's blueberries, apple pies with the dried apples in the pantry, and rhubarb pies with the new summer rhubarb.

Bo hated rhubarb—slimy, horrible stuff. But lots of people said that was their very favorite kind of pie. When she was little, Bo used to be surprised that people didn't like the things she liked and liked things she hated.

"It's not in nature for people to all like the same things," Jack told her. "What you always got to do when you're the cook is make sure there are plenty of choices. That way you're safe. Don't got to listen to whining."

That's why he made four kinds of pies so everyone could have the kind they liked best. When they were all baked, he set them on the pantry shelf and covered them with a cloth. That was one job done for the Fourth of July.

The next day, he started the doughnuts. When the first two hundred were done, he tossed them in the big bowl with sugar, and that was the doughnuts done for that day. Bo must put them in big tins to keep them fresh, stacking them carefully so they wouldn't get squashed. The next day, Jack made another batch because there would be a lot of people at the Fourth of July, and doughnuts were what they looked forward to all year. Four hundred doughnuts were not too many.

The boys all knew when Jack was making doughnuts. "Can smell them all the way to the tailing piles," Lester said. So they came into the cookshack when they got a chance and raided the tins.

"Nothing like fresh doughnuts, nothing in this world," said Alex. "If there's a heaven, which I doubt, it'll be fresh doughnuts every day, many as you want."

ON THE FOURTH OF JULY, everyone gathered at the grass field by the riverbank. Bo and Jack brought the doughnut tins to town in a wheelbarrow, and when they got there, Jack tumbled the doughnuts into a big galvanized tub so everyone could help themselves while they watched the fun. Four hundred doughnuts fit just right in the tub.

The races for the kids were first. Bo and Oscar

couldn't win any of them, because the other kids were much older. Only Evalina was slower than they were because she was just four. But Bo and Oscar got in all the races, anyway. They didn't care if they never won.

There were three-legged races and gunny-sack races for everyone, kids and grown-ups together. And wheelbarrow races, which Bo hated because the one who was the wheelbarrow had to walk on his hands. So Oscar always did that.

Arm wrestling was next, and of course Jack and Arvid couldn't be beat, so they had to wrestle each other. Sometimes Jack won, and sometimes Arvid won. But they were the only miners who won anything.

Sammy won the knife-throwing contest; Big Annie won the target shoot again; and Della won the wood-chopping contest. She beat Philipe and Lester easily. The boys slapped their thighs and bent double teasing Philipe and Lester. "Fourteen!

Fourteen years old, and a girl at that!" they chortled. But Philipe and Lester were good sports and picked Della up and rode her around on their shoulders while everyone cheered.

The most exciting race was the footrace, all across the field by the river, around the roadhouse, and back. Milo said it was just a little over a mile.

The boys from the mine were left in the dust. Charlie Sickik, Oscar's father, and Budu, Atok's father, were faster than any of them. "Well, stands to reason," Milo told Arvid. "Those guys walk hundreds of miles in the spring and the fall after the caribou, and another hundred going uphill after the sheep. Our Eskimos is tough."

After the games and races, everyone went home to put on their best clothes and to get the food they'd cooked for the big dinner—fried rabbit and spruce hen, caribou dry meat and smoked salmon from last summer, roasted caribou and sheep, and moose soup. There were bowls of macaroni and rice, last year's blueberries and cranberries, mashed potatoes, and a huge pile of bannocks Gitnoo had made. And of course seal oil.

The women had set the long table with fifty places and had decorated the walls with flags and red, white, and blue bunting. It looked beautiful.

The first thing Bo did was drop cranberries on her new pink dress, which made a dreadful stain. She looked up quickly to see if Lilly had noticed.

"Don't worry," Jack whispered to her. "It's not ruined. Little vinegar'll take care of that spot."

While they were eating, the speeches started. Big Jim started them off, and then Milo, Jimmy the Pirate, Siwash George, and Budu had their say, and still there were more speeches to come. Bo wondered why it was always the men who made speeches.

When Bo and Oscar had eaten everything they could eat, they slipped down from their chairs and crawled under the table, in the middle where no one could kick them. "Too much talking," Oscar said. The speeches went on for a while, and Bo and Oscar went to sleep until it was time for dessert.

Jack got up and cut all the pies in eight pieces and passed them down the table. Nakuchluk brought out two big bowls of akutaq and passed those around as well.

While everyone was eating dessert, people would call out for songs. Tomas Kovish loved to be invited to sing. He sang sad songs about things like birds, and his voice wobbled in an interesting way.

Lester and Bo were called on to do their best song. Lester had taught Bo how to look frightened: she swept her arms out at the side, held her hands by her mouth, made a round mouth like an o, and opened her eyes very wide, like the lady in the music hall had done. Bo loved doing that. Arvid said she was a natural-born ham.

Everyone knew Lester and Bo's song, so they sang the chorus with them:

Oh, don't go in the lion's cage tonight, Mother darling,
For the lion looks ferocious and may bite.
When he gets his angry fits,
He may tear you all to bits!
Oh, don't go in the lion's cage tonight!

Then Big Jim, Dinuk, and Charlie Sickik went to the storeroom and brought out their drums. Big Jim's was almost as big as he was, but the others had the smaller drums.

"Eskimo turn now!" cried Big Jim.

Unakserak and Budu and the rest of the Eskimo men jumped up to dance to the drumming, along with two young ones, Sammy and Peluk, who'd been learning the dances from Big Jim most of the winter.

Then the women made a line in front of the men. They stood still in one spot, their feet neatly together, and moved just their hands and arms, perfectly matching each other's movements.

The men's dancing was much more energetic. They jumped and crouched and made powerful gestures. Everyone cheered the most for Unakserak, who looked fierce and dangerous while he danced.

The drumming made Bo feel all wild inside. She wanted to jump up and dance, too. She would ask Big Jim if he would teach her the dances.

Then the women cleared the plates and dishes, and the men pushed the tables back against the wall. It was time for everyone to dance.

Bo danced two times with Oscar and once with Jonas, though his mother, Gracie, had to make him dance with Bo. Jonas said he was eight and didn't like to dance with *little* girls. She danced with Lester and Peter and Johnny, and then Arvid asked for a polka so he could teach Bo how to do it. Everyone lined up and swept all the way down the length of the roadhouse and back again, twirling and twisting and stomping. That polka was the most fun of all.

Jack loved to dance, but all the women said he was a terrible dancer.

"Too big! You step on my toes, you break them," Clara teased him. So they only danced the slow songs with him, when he wouldn't be moving so fast, and they could get out of his way if he got dangerous.

Jack said it wasn't his fault; it was Mama Nancy's.

"She wouldn't let anyone in the cookhouse dance. She said dancing was the devil's way of getting your attention," he said.

So the people of Ballard Creek danced all night in the golden summer light, and that was another Fourth of July.

CHAPTER SIXTEEN

GOING TO FAIRBANKS

ALL OF SUMMER was spent getting ready for winter. Summer wasn't very long, but it seemed longer, because the sun stayed up all day and all night. Since it never grew dark in the summer, everyone worked hard all hours of the day and night. It seemed to Bo as if no one in the little town *ever* slept in the summer.

In the winter there were just a few hours of sunlight. Everyone was in a hurry then to get chores finished before it grew dark and you couldn't see what you were doing. You make a lot of mistakes in the dark, Arvid always said.

Bo had to hurry to bring in the snow to melt in the water barrel and the wood for the wood box. You're burning daylight, they'd say if you wasted time in the winter.

But in the summer, there was nothing but daylight.

There wasn't much time between cleanup and the new season when the ground froze again. When the freeze-up came, it would be safe for the boys to go underground again to dig for gold.

The boys worked hard at getting the equipment ready for the winter. Arvid and Alex had taken apart the pump, the buzz saw, the boiler, and the winch, replacing worn parts and cleaning everything carefully. The rocker had to be fixed, the hoses dried and put away, the ladder for the shaft repaired. There was wood to be cut and new handles had to be made for the picks and shovels.

But some of the boys had other things to do in the summer. They were going to leave on the scow out of Ballard Creek after breakfast. This happened every summer, but it always made Bo unhappy when any of the boys left Ballard Creek.

Peter had a bad tooth so he was going down the

Koyukuk to catch a steamer from Nulato to Fairbanks, where there was a dentist. Bo leaned against Peter's shoulder while he sat on the bench lacing up his boots.

Peter looked at her sad face. "I'll bring you some new rocks," he told Bo. Bo frowned to show him that she couldn't be cheered up with rocks.

"Where will you sleep when you're in Fairbanks?" she asked.

"Oh, everyone stays in the Nordale Hotel. Got an elevator in that." Bo didn't really know what an elevator was, so Peter said he'd draw her a picture when he finished with his boots.

Johnny Schmidt was going Outside. That's what everyone called all the places outside Alaska. He was going Outside to see his old parents in Oregon. They had a farm there, and he was worried because they were getting too old to farm by themselves. He said he would be back on the last scow, but Bo thought the boys said good-bye to him as if it were the last time they'd see him. Jack shook his hand a lot longer than he usually did. When Johnny bent to kiss Bo good-bye, it felt to her as if he was going for good, and she burst into tears.

Even Charlie Sickik, Big Annie's husband, was going to Fairbanks. He had a bad tooth too. All winter he suffered, drinking whiskey when it hurt too bad. Milo wired the dentist in Fairbanks to see if he could just pull Charlie's tooth out himself with his pliers, but the dentist said no because Charlie's face was swollen. Charlie had to come to see him.

Charlie was very excited about going to Fairbanks. He'd never been away from the Koyukuk River in his whole life. He talked and talked about all the things he was going to see—automobiles and airplanes and electric lights and telephones, and the new locomotive going to Anchorage. Little Annie and Betty, his twins, made him promise he'd go to see the talkies, that new kind of movies, so he could tell them all what it was like. But when the old-timers and the boys told Charlie terrible stories about dentists, he almost changed his mind about going. Milo had to talk hard to convince him that it wasn't going to be so bad.

Karl was going to Fairbanks too. "Just want to see the bright lights of the city," he said, and all the boys laughed, because Fairbanks wasn't a city, and there weren't any bright lights. Fairbanks was just a little mining town with a few thousand people. Which was a lot more people than Ballard Creek had, of course.

Bo knew why Karl was really going. It was because of old Nels Niemi.

Everyone knew the story of Nels Niemi. The boys all smiled about it, but Karl didn't, and neither did Bo.

Everyone worried about the miners out on the creeks who worked all by themselves. They had no one to go for help if they got sick or hurt.

Karl was Finnish and so was Nels, so Karl looked after Nels. "Us Finns got to stick together," he said. They'd talk Finnish together when Karl visited, just so they didn't forget how. "Easy to forget a language when you don't use it," Karl told Bo. "Take Arvid—he don't hardly know Swedish anymore, just the swear words." So Karl took Nels some of Jack's bread every few weeks, brought him his mail, and checked to see that he was okay.

Every year Nels left Ballard Creek with the gold

he'd cleaned up at his little mine a few miles from Olaf's. Every year Nels said he was going to see his sister in Washington. He hadn't seen her for twenty-five years, and she was the only family he had left. She wrote all the time, begging him to visit. Nels always told her he was coming.

And every year when he got to Fairbanks, he lost all his money in a card game or some other foolishness and came back to Ballard Creek shamefaced. "I'll go see her next year," he always said.

Karl didn't have any family at all, so he felt bad when Nels didn't make it to see his sister. "If you have a sister, you should do your best for her, show up once in a while, send a letter for her birthday at least," he complained to the boys after his last visit with Nels.

The last time it happened, the year before, Bo had been old enough to feel sad with Karl. "Think how his sister must feel," Karl said to Bo. She thought it would be terrible to wait all those times and never see her brother. She thought it was mean of Nels to hurt his sister's feelings.

So this year Karl was going with Nels to keep

him out of trouble and to get him on the boat to his sister.

KARL AND NELS had been gone two weeks when Clarence brought a wire to the boss. All the boys were together in the cookshack having lunch, and they stopped eating when the boss said, "It's from Karl."

The boss fished his wire-rimmed glasses out of his shirt pocket and took forever adjusting the wires behind his ears. The boys were rolling their eyes with impatience. Finally he cleared his throat and read the wire to them.

> *He's on his way. I took his money and wired it to his sister. That way he can't get into any card games on the boat. Not too much trouble he can get into with what's in his pocket. She's going to let me know when he gets there.*

The boys all cheered. Bo smiled at Arvid and leaned against him. It made her happy, thinking of Nels finally seeing his sister. She imagined Nels's sister looking like Olaf's sister Birgit, with braids around her head, and she imagined how Nels's sister would cry when she saw Nels. And how they would talk a lot of Finnish.

"By god," said Sandor, "I knew Karl could pull it off."

Alex said, "What do you think Karl had to do to get Nels's money off him?" The boys all thought up ways Karl could have managed it until they were all laughing so hard they almost forgot to eat. They weren't too sure that Nels wouldn't find some kind of mischief to get up to, but at least he was halfway there.

KARL DIDN'T STAY long in Fairbanks. He was on the next scow that came up from Bettles.

The night he returned, when everyone was at the roadhouse, Karl handed out presents from his battered old duffel bag.

"Just like Santa Claus," Milo said.

There were pipes for all the grown-ups in town and fat cigars for the boys who didn't smoke pipes. There were store-bought kites and candy for all the kids, boxes of ribbons for the big girls, and balsa wood airplane kits for the big boys to put together with glue and tissue. And best of all, there were new records for the roadhouse.

"These are the latest hits," Karl told the big girls. They read the titles on the records excitedly—"Yes We Have No Bananas," "I've Got Rings on My Fingers," and "Toot, Toot, Tootsie." The girls rushed to the Victrola, arguing over who got to pick the first record.

When he had finished handing out all these things, Karl called Bo and Evalina to him. "You are the two youngest girls, so I brought something special for you," he said. He pulled two boxes from his duffel bag, looking very pleased. In the boxes were dolls, beautiful dolls with glossy hair and shiny faces and eyes that opened and shut. He took the dolls out of the boxes and handed the doll with blond hair to Bo and the one with red hair to Evalina.

"This one has hair like you," he said to Bo.

"Couldn't find one with black hair like you, Evalina, but you have one with hair like Lester."

Bo felt a terrible feeling she'd never felt before.

She wanted the doll with red hair like Lester.

Bo and Evalina stood stiff legged, holding their dolls awkwardly, their eyes down. Karl looked at Bo and then at Evalina and then back to Bo again. His happy face changed as he watched them. The big girls, Little Annie, Betty, Della, and Lena, leaned over Bo and Evalina to look at the dolls.

"Oh, aren't they beautiful!" Lena breathed.

But still Bo and Evalina stood rigid.

Bo looked out of the corners of her eyes at Evalina.

Evalina was looking sideways at Bo's doll with the yellow hair.

Karl watched them, frowning, and then his face cleared. "Ohhhhh," he said in a discovering sort of way. He squatted down and took both dolls back again.

"Here, I've made a mistake," he said. "I forgot to let you choose. Evalina, you're the youngest, so you get to pick first. Which one do you want?"

Evalina threw a worried look at Bo. Finally she whispered, "The one with yellow hair."

Bo's smile was radiant.

"Yes," she said to Evalina. "That's the best one for you." She took the red-haired doll from Karl quickly, afraid Evalina'd change her mind. She smiled her biggest smile and put her hand on Karl's knee.

"Thank you for our dolls. Thank you." She nudged Evalina who was gazing adoringly at her yellow-haired doll. "Say your manners," she whispered.

"Thank you," Evalina said.

Karl got to his feet and raised his eyebrows a little at the boys who were watching. "Whew," he said.

THAT NIGHT when Bo was washed and ready for bed, Arvid sat on the rickety chair by the door and pulled Bo between his big knees. He looked into her face. "What do you think about the doll Karl got you?"

Bo knew that Arvid had seen her behaving badly. She looked at the floor. "I wanted the one like Lester," she said.

"Oh," said Arvid. "That's a hard thing. Wanting what someone else has. Get jealous when someone has something you want. I guess there ain't anyone that never happened to. Best when that happens to talk yourself into thinking that what you have is good enough. Worked out okay, because Evalina wanted to swap."

Bo looked up at him. "She wanted the one with hair like me."

Arvid nodded.

"When I was five or six, the boy next door got a jackknife. I was real jealous. So I stole it."

Bo's eyes went wide. "You stole?"

"Mama caught me, made me give it back, gave me a good talking to," said Arvid. "She read me this place in the Bible says you shouldn't want what your neighbor has. I hated it when she read the Bible at me. I didn't want my neighbor's cow or his donkey, and I sure didn't want his wife, since he didn't have one any more than I did, because we weren't even in long pants yet. I wanted his jackknife."

Bo looked up at Arvid and let herself smile. Arvid always made jokes about everything. Even though she tried to stay unhappy, he always made that bad heavy place inside her feel lighter.

"I think Mama felt worse than I did. On my next birthday, she gave me a jackknife, better than that boy's knife! That's mothers for you. Can't be too hard on their children. By rights she should have told me I could never in this life have my own knife because I stole."

Bo relaxed against Arvid's knee. It was a good thing to know that someone else had done the bad thing you'd done. She hadn't stolen the doll, of course, but she might have.

"I never forgot what it felt like, being jealous. Worst feeling in the world. The thing is not to want things, just be happy with what you got." Arvid tilted her chin up with his big finger. "I know. Easier said than done. I myself couldn't help being very jealous if someone had a little girl like you and I didn't have any little girl."

CHAPTER SEVENTEEN
GETTING READY
FOR WINTER

THE ESKIMO FAMILIES worked hard all summer getting food for the long cold winter. The
women did most of the fishing, and the men were
gone most of the summer hunting caribou because
the caribou migration passed through the hill country north of Ballard Creek twice a year. After the
caribou were gone, the men went off to hunt wild
sheep in the mountains fifty miles away.

Jack had seen a caribou migration. He told Bo
there might be ten thousand caribou all running
together.

"How much is ten thousand?" Bo asked.

"A lot," said Jack. "Maybe if they were jammed together they'd stretch all the way to Olaf's."

Bo tried to imagine such a crowd.

"Caribou click when they run," Jack said. "Darnedest thing you could ever hear. All those caribou, running together, not saying a word, just *clickclickclick*."

"How do they make a click?" asked Bo. She was imagining the caribou making clicks with their tongues the way Olaf called his animals.

"Don't know," said Jack. "Something with their legs. Something in there clicking."

Jack said sometimes the migration went someplace else. For almost twenty years there were no caribou in the Koyukuk country. "But they came back," said Jack, "and a good thing, too."

Bo longed to see a caribou migration. And hear it.

Oscar loved fresh caribou meat. "Best thing," Oscar told her, "is the big intestine. But my dad and mom, they like the heart, tongue, and liver best. Brain, too."

Bo didn't like the idea of any of those things. She didn't even know what some of them were; she just knew they were inside the caribou. Jack would never cook the insides of anything, she knew.

Oscar liked stinkfish, too, and that was another thing Bo didn't like. But when the whitefish run was over, she went to help Clara make stinkfish anyway.

Clara had dug a deep, narrow hole close to their cabin. She used the same hole every year for her stinkfish.

While Clara went off to load the fish on her sled, Bo and Oscar knelt by the side of the hole and looked down with interest.

"Let's see what it feels like down there," Oscar said. Bo thought that was a good idea. She sat on the edge of the hole and jumped down feet first. Oscar came after. There was just enough room for both of them. "Didn't look as deep from up there," said Bo. They looked up at the patch of sky over their heads.

"We'd never get out if we were stuck down here by ourself," Bo said.

"Sure," said Oscar. "Just have to dig little holes for steps, and you could climb out, just like you made a ladder." So they tried to make holes with their fingers, but the sides of the pit were frozen too hard.

"Should always carry a knife with you," said Oscar.

"Get on my shoulders," said Bo. "Then you could climb right out." They tried that, but it didn't work. Although Oscar was shorter than Bo, he was heavier, and Bo went to her knees every time Oscar tried to climb on her shoulders. Bo got on Oscar's shoulders then, but she couldn't reach high enough.

It was cold in that hole, and there was still some of last year's fish in it, so they both got smeared with old rotten fish. Bo had a feeling Jack was not going to like that.

They were both thinking that jumping into the hole was not their best idea when Clara's face appeared.

Clara laughed at them. "Oh, my, what were you thinking of?" Then she reached down with her strong arms to pull them out. "Getting heavy, you two," she complained.

She gave Oscar a sharp knife and sent them both off to the riverbank to gather grass and willow branches to cover the bottom of the hole. When they'd done that, Clara and Bo and Oscar brought the whitefish from the sled. They were big fish, so Oscar and Bo couldn't hold them by the gills; they had to hug them to carry them. They slid the whitefish into the pit, piling them on top of each other until the hole was full. Clara covered the top of the hole with grass and sod, and then it was done. They just had to wait until the fish were rotten so they could eat it.

When Bo got home that night, Jack took one look at her, made a face, and told her to get back on the porch.

"Take your clothes off," he ordered. "Don't want that smell in the cookshack. Put everyone off their food for sure."

He got down the galvanized tub from its nail on the wall, filled it with hot water, and set the tub in front of the stove. Then he brought her into the kitchen, his nose wrinkled, and popped her into the bathtub. He used a lot of soap.

"I thought you didn't like stinkfish," he said while he scrubbed her.

"I didn't *eat* any. I was just helping Clara," Bo said.

Jack rolled his eyes. "What next?" he said.

CHAPTER EIGHTEEN

FALL

ALL THE MEN who'd gone to Fairbanks in the summer had stories to tell when they came back.

Charlie Sickik hadn't seen the talkies, because they hadn't come to Fairbanks yet.

"But I went to the movies at the Empress Theater. Had a guy there who played the piano and one guy who read what the words said on the big screen. It was all about these robbers getting away from the cops. Pretty good, those movies."

Charlie had seen automobiles in Fairbanks, but he didn't think much of them.

"Lot of noise and got to wind it up, and it goes a little bit—bump, bump—then it tips over in a hole or something, got to start it all over again. Bump, bump. No good," he said.

He and Karl had gone together to see the new train that came to Fairbanks, and they'd gone to the ball field and looked at all the airplanes. They both thought Fairbanks was way too noisy. For one thing there was this siren that blew from the Northern Commercial Company every noon.

"Every dog in town, hundreds of dogs—more than people—they howl when the noon siren goes off. And then they howl some more when the train whistle blows. Howlingest place I ever saw. Couldn't hear yourself think. Don't know how they stand it, them people," Karl said.

Johnny Schmidt didn't come back. He sent a wire to the boss to say he'd have to stay at home to help the old folks. The boys were quiet when the boss read them that wire, and Bo's throat closed up with rough, hard tears.

Arvid saw how she looked, and he said quickly, "Thing to do is write to Johnny. You tell me what you want to say, I'll write it out. Send him a letter and tell him all about everything. And he'll write back, and that way you won't miss him so much."

Bo looked down at her plate, but right away she started thinking about what she'd tell Johnny in her letter, and she felt a little better.

Nels Niemi came back on the last scow, and he brought his sister with him.

She was a little gray-haired lady dressed in men's overalls and boots, who smiled all the time. Bo was so excited that she pushed through the crowd around the scow and took the little woman's hand. Bo couldn't say anything, she was so happy to see Nels's sister.

"This here is Bo," Nels said. "And these are her papas. Meet my sister Asa," he said. Asa looked a little startled when she shook hands with Arvid and Jack.

Asa got a big greeting from everyone, just like Bo did when she came to town. Asa'd never been anywhere in her life besides her hometown.

The boys couldn't get over her. "Imagine that little woman being so skookum. Just jumped up and come to the middle of nowhere, six days on the scow, gnats driving everyone nuts, walking all the way out to the creek with Nels. Don't find little old ladies like that just anywhere."

"Not letting Nels out of her sight this time," Alex said.

"He's going to have it good now," Sandor said. "Got a partner who can cook. Can't beat that."

Miss Sylvia, the teacher, missed the last scow when she was coming back from her summer vacation. She sent a wire to Budu and Dinuk and so they went to Bettles to pick her up. They brought her up the Koyukuk in their poling boat. The water was so low, Budu and Dinuk had to neck it most of the way. Necking was when you waded through the water or along the bank, pulling the boat with two long ropes. They were proud it took them only six days to come from Bettles.

Miss Sylvia was a jolly, round-faced woman with

short graying hair like women in the
Montgomery Ward catalog. She
had round glasses that made her
blue eyes look very big. She'd
taught at Ballard Creek since
before Bo came, but she'd taught
in lots of other places, too. She said
she never had such smart students, ever, as her students in Ballard Creek.

Everyone liked her very much. Some of the
grown-ups had gone to the mission school when they
were children, but they said Miss Sylvia's school was
much better. At the mission school, they had learned
nothing but the catechism and the Bible verses, which
they didn't think were very useful.

Bo asked Jack what the catechism was, but he
said he didn't know. Some church thing, he thought.

Miss Sylvia never taught the catechism or the
Bible verses.

School would start soon, and all the children
would be going except Bo, Kapuk, who was just a
baby, and Evalina.

Even Oscar would be going. There would be no
Oscar to play with in the bright fall sun or to go

with to the roadhouse to read magazines. Arvid and Jack tried to get her used to the idea, but Bo couldn't even imagine what it would be like not to have Oscar with her all the time.

"It's not that long," Jack said. "He goes in the morning, be home for lunch. You could visit him then. And he'll be out in the afternoon. Not too late. Three o'clock, I think. You'll have all day after that to see Oscar."

But Bo said that it would be dark when Oscar got out of school, and he'd have chores to do. "Well, there's Saturday and Sunday, too," they pointed out.

Everything in her life had been the same, year after year. And now it was going to change.

ON THE DAY SCHOOL started, Bo and Evalina went inside with the other children, just to visit for a bit. They were both feeling left out. Oscar was sitting in the front row with the youngest children. He looked so happy to be there, his face scrubbed and shiny. He was wearing the new overalls that Arvid had made him.

There were fourteen students in the school—and not just kids. Atok's grandma was starting the second grade, and Dinuk was in the third grade, just like his son Jonas. The grown-ups were happy to be learning. They'd never had a chance to go to school when they were young.

The little school was pretty crowded. Everyone sat on benches facing the teacher's desk. And they all looked shiny like Oscar.

There was a blackboard and an American flag at the front of the room, and all over the room there were pictures of wonderful things.

Above the blackboard there was a long row of the alphabet, big letters and little ones, and under the alphabet were all the numbers to one hundred. That was one thing she was glad about. She didn't have to learn all those numbers yet.

They began with a song, and then they stood up to say something to the flag on the wall, their hands on their chests. They all seemed to know it by heart. Except Oscar. Bo could see Oscar was just pretending to say it because he'd never heard it before. Bo didn't know what the words meant.

Bo and Evalina stayed until that was over, and then they knew it was time for them to go. Bo threw a look at Oscar, and then she took Evalina's hand, and they walked out of the school together, feeling very sad.

Miss Sylvia called after them. "Here," she said, smiling. She gave each girl a new box of crayons. Bo could tell that Miss Sylvia knew they were sad, so she smiled back at her.

"Thank you," she said.

"Thank you too much," said Evalina.

But still. A box of new crayons didn't really make up for Oscar.

CHAPTER NINETEEN
THE CAT

ONE SATURDAY in early winter, Bo and Oscar and most of the other children were in the road-house. They were waiting for Gus Ostnes to bring his Cat to Ballard Creek.

They were so jittery and restless that Milo threatened to throw them out in the snow if they didn't settle down. They wouldn't take their parkas off because they wanted to be able to run out the door without waiting a minute.

A Cat was what they called a big Caterpillar

tractor, which was a very new thing. It ran on gas just like airplanes and automobiles. Jack showed Bo a picture of one in a magazine and told her how it crawled along like a caterpillar on big rubber treads. "That's why a Cat can go places a thing with wheels can never go," Jack said.

Gus Ostnes had bought his Cat last year in Fairbanks and shipped it to Bettles. He was going to be a freighter. He'd bring the things people needed over the old winter trail to Ballard Creek. Now the only way to move goods in the winter was by dog team, and the sleds couldn't carry anything heavy. The Cat could haul more than twenty sleds could carry in one trip. Everyone's lives would change when they could get freight in the winter.

But the Cat kept breaking down, and Gus had to keep ordering parts for it. The men of Ballard Creek and Bettles had worried about that all last winter. This year was better, though. There wasn't too much snow, and the Cat seemed to be running fine. So Gus had wired ahead that he was coming and to look for him if he didn't show up in two days.

The children had come to the roadhouse way too early. Milo said it would be ages before the Cat came. He said they'd be able to hear it from far, far away, it was so rackety.

Every once in a while, Oscar or Jonas would jump up and poke his head out the door of the roadhouse to see if he could hear it. In the meantime, they sat on the floor with their backs against the bar, legs stretched out, reading magazines.

Bo and Oscar were together reading the same magazine, as usual. Bo started whistling.

Oscar had been teaching Bo how to whistle, and she practiced a lot. She practiced so much that she didn't even know she was doing it anymore.

Oscar punched her with his elbow. "Stop," he growled.

"Oh, sorry," said Bo. "Jack says he'll go crazy if I don't stop whistling. He says I should at least whistle a tune. But I don't know how to make it go into a tune."

Oscar gave her a look but didn't offer to teach her about whistling tunes.

They were reading a *National Geographic* magazine, their favorite because it had the best pictures. Oscar liked to see the naked people because they were so different from the naked people he saw all the time. Bo too, because she'd never seen any naked people except in the *National Geographic*.

Suddenly they could hear someone's feet pounding up the porch stairs and then Manuluk jerked open the door.

"Cat coming! Cat coming!"

All the children dropped their magazines and scrambled out the door with Milo right after them.

They could hear the Cat as soon as they got out the door. Nothing else sounded like that. It was different from the airplane. Growlier.

"Bet he's at Marion Creek," said Milo. That was seven miles away.

All the kids in town were running, heading for the trail. "Let's go!" yelled Sammy. He was the biggest boy, and he bossed everyone around.

Bo and Oscar were in the back of the pack of children. Bo thought they all looked like swallows swooping across the river.

The winter trail was firmly packed and perfect. The sun was shining, and the sky was a hard blue. It was nice to run with her new mukluks down the trail, the dry snow crunching at each step. The rabbits that ran from them were nearly all white, and so were the ptarmigan they surprised, pecking for pebbles under the light snow cover.

They ran for a long time. They only stopped to grab some snow to eat because they were thirsty, or they'd stop a second to listen for the Cat.

It got closer and closer, louder and louder. They had reached Dry Gulch, where Ollie Deglar mined a little in the summer. Dry Gulch was three miles from Ballard Creek.

Suddenly the Cat sounded so loud, so close, that they were terrified to stay on the trail. Maybe it would run over them. They all darted into the bushes by the side of the trail as Gus and the Cat came over the top of a little hill.

Bo screamed and screamed—they all did. She didn't know if she was happy or afraid. Gus stopped the big monster and climbed down, laughing and shaking his head.

"All the way to Dry Gulch," he said. "I bet you could run to Bettles no problem, you bunch of savages." He took off his wool hat and tied the flaps on top to be out of the way. "It's warm up there on top of that engine," he said. Then he swept his arm back. "Climb aboard."

They all stood still for a moment. They hadn't known for sure that Gus would give them a ride. The littlest ones, he said, could sit up with him in the driver's seat. He showed Bo and Oscar where to put their feet on those big bands and gave them a boost up to the seat. Ekok and Jonas had a bit of a wrestle to decide who would sit next to Gus and the big stick with a knob on top.

The older kids could ride on the go-devil. That's what he called the big sled that he pulled behind. It was piled with boxes of freight for the roadhouse store. Della, Manuluk, Sammy, Lena, Annie, Betty, and the rest arranged themselves on the go-devil, sitting on boxes and barrels or between them. Gus looked at Sammy seriously.

"You're the oldest. Anything goes wrong back there, you let me know." Sammy looked very proud.

And then they bumped and bounced three miles over the winter trail back to Ballard Creek. They couldn't talk or they'd bite their tongues, so they just looked at each other with shining faces.

Gus drove the Cat all the way to the roadhouse, where everyone in town was waiting for him. They all helped unload the go-devil and bring the boxes

into the roadhouse while Milo fed Gus a big plate of stew and dumplings. Gus was to stay overnight at the roadhouse and start back to Bettles in the morning.

The kids were all so wild and noisy that Milo had to threaten again that he'd throw them in the snowbank if they didn't quiet down. So they ran outside and climbed all over the Cat, taking turns pretending they were driving until they were greasy and covered with filthy slush from the big treads and their mamas sent them home.

CHAPTER TWENTY

WINTER

AFTER THE CAT had gone, the children were wishing for a heavy snow to fall because they wanted to go sliding on the riverbank. But the bad cold set in then—thirty and forty below— and it wouldn't snow again until it warmed up.

Nearly everyone liked winter best. You couldn't walk around the country in the summer very easily, not with the tundra and grass lakes and sedge tussocks. In the summer, you had to travel by boat unless there was a really good trail.

In the winter, you could go everywhere—on the frozen rivers, on the trails, across country. At least until the snow got so deep you'd be swimming in it. Deep snow was not good for walking or for dog teams, but you could walk on the deep snow with snowshoes.

When it was cold, you could freeze your meat and anything else outdoors—loaves of extra bread, cakes, cookies. And anytime you wanted, you could make ice cream.

Of course the cold was good for drift mining.

The boys were back underground, this time making some new tunnels off the shaft, trying to find some richer ground than they'd had the last few years.

JACK GOT ALL their heavy winter clothes out of the storage shed. He and Arvid both wore size-fifteen boots, great heavy leather shoe packs. Bo loved to put on their boots and try to lift her feet off the floor. They came up to her thighs and couldn't be budged. She couldn't even scoot them, they were so heavy, and when she tried, she just fell over.

Frost spread up the windows of the cookshack in beautiful lacy patterns. She mustn't touch the frost or breathe on it, or the lace would be ruined.

The beautiful frost pictures didn't last long. It got colder—forty, fifty below on the cookshack thermometer—and the frost patterns became thick stubborn lumps of ice. Too cold to snow.

Jack lit the extra stove in the cookshack, the one he'd made from an oil drum. The cookshack needed two stoves going when it got that cold. At night, he'd fill the stove with birch because it would burn longer than spruce and he wouldn't have to get up at night to put in more wood.

Bo liked to hear the stove crackling first thing in the morning while she and Bear were still warm in her bed. Jack would tap on the stovepipe to knock down the creosote, then scrape the red coals from back to front. She knew just what he would do next—lay the kindling on top of those coals, and then the split spruce, and then she'd hear the scree of the damper as he turned it to just the right opening. When she could hear the fire roaring, he'd call.

"Nice and warm now! Get your clothes and get dressed by the stove."

The dark lasted a long time now and came earlier in the afternoon. Every day after she did the dishes, Gitnoo washed the soot from the lamp chimneys, trimmed the wicks, and filled the bowls with coal oil.

The northern lights were out every night, a cold white curtain tumbling and sliding across the starry black sky. Sometimes they would be a little pink or green as well.

"Once, long time ago, I saw the red northern lights," Arvid told Bo. "Not just a little red, but really red, just as red as blood. Prettiest thing I ever saw." Bo longed to see red northern lights.

Big Annie would hook up her dog team every other day to go check her traplines. Sometimes she'd take Bo and Evalina, too, because they were the only two big children not in school and Annie felt sorry for them.

Big Annie would dress Evalina in her warmest

clothes, and then she'd drive the dogs over the bridge to the cookshack to get Bo. Then Jack would dress Bo in her warmest clothes: long wool underwear, wool overall pants with a bib, and canvas pants on top so that the snow wouldn't stick to the wool. Then a parka with the fur turned inside, and sometimes, in the worst cold, a parka cover to go over that.

Gracie, Jonas's mother, had made Bo's parka out of siksikpuk, the marmots that lived in the hills. It took a lot of them to make a parka, even a little one like Bo's. Unakserak was too old to go hunting for caribou, but in the spring he always snared siksikpuk for parkas.

Bo's parka had a wolverine and wolf fur ruff to keep the wind from her face.

And last was a pair of moose-hide mitts with a long harness to keep them from getting lost and a pair of moose-hide boots with caribou socks inside and her thick wool socks that Lilly had knitted for her.

You needed a lot of clothes in the winter.

Bo hated getting dressed in her cold-weather clothes, because before she was half finished, she'd be so hot she could hardly stand it. She'd have to dash outdoors for a minute to cool off and then come back in for another layer.

Jack was very careful about dressing her properly. "Nearly froze to death when I first came into the country. I'll never forget what that felt like. I was so young and so dumb, didn't know anything about the cold, being from Louisiana."

When he pulled the overparka on top of all the other layers, Bo looked as round and fat as Gitnoo.

Big Annie would settle Bo and Evalina in the dogsled, and off they'd go, Annie riding the runners and kicking hard. Bo and Evalina loved going with Annie. They never got cold, and even when the sled tipped over and threw them out on the trail, they were so padded with clothes they didn't get hurt a bit.

But Bo didn't like seeing the dead marten Big Annie caught, so she turned her face away while Annie was taking them out of her traps.

One day Bo woke up to find that it had warmed up during the night and the frost was slowly melting, running onto the windowsills. Jack shut down the drum stove because they didn't need two stoves now.

"It's going to snow, I just know it!" Bo said

"Yep, warm enough to snow for sure," Jack said.

And the sky grew gray, the soft lovely color of pussy willows, and down fell the big soft flakes, tumbling out of the sky.

Bo stuck out her tongue to catch them, and when they landed on her parka, she could see all their beautiful shapes.

It was a beautiful snow, heavy and wet, and it lasted for three days. A thin stack of snow teetered on each branch of the birch and aspen trees. When Bo shook the trees, the snow would fall straight down off the branches with a good sound. *Shlump!*

At the end of the three days, the riverbank was covered with a beautiful layer of pure white snow, and they could begin sliding. Everyone came out, grown-ups and all, because sliding was not just for kids.

Everyone who had a sled took turns with the ones who didn't have one. They all liked Bo's little

sled, which Jack and Arvid had
made last year. It went fast because
it had iron runners. The big boys
would throw themselves belly
down on her sled and use
their hands to push faster.

But you didn't really
need a real sled. Nakuchluk
gave them a stiff dried caribou skin. That's what
she had used when she was little and she said it was
better than a sled. And maybe it *was* best of all,
because lots of kids could pile onto it.

They got cold when it was almost dark, so they
went to the roadhouse, where the grown-ups drank
coffee and Milo made the kids cocoa.

Even though it was dark by then, they went back
outside and slid down some more.

When Bo came home from the riverbank, she
was covered with powdered snow, and her eyelashes
and the tips of her ruff were all frosted. She was so
tired that she fell asleep while Jack was getting her
into her pajamas.

CHAPTER TWENTY-ONE
MAIL SLED

EVERYONE IN BALLARD CREEK knew the mail sled was on its way when all the dogs in town started to howl. The dogs could hear the little bells Max put on the harnesses of his sled dogs long before any of the people in town could hear a thing.

They were all happy when the winter mail started to come. They could always count on it. Max came seven times in the winter, cross-country from Nenana, only a short run on a good trail. Jack showed Bo on the map.

"See, trail starts in Nenana, just like the boats,

but Max cuts across the Yukon here, up-country, turns left here for Ballard Creek. Just four hundred some miles."

In the summer, the mail traveled three times as many miles on the rivers, and you couldn't tell when anything would get through, what with the ice breaking up and the flooding, fires, and water too low or too high. One summer they didn't get any mail at all—until the very last scow in the fall.

In the winter, Max almost always got through, no matter how cold or how bad the trail. He prided himself on that.

Max stopped his team by the side of the road-house where the dog barns were.

"How's the trail?" Milo yelled from the doorway of the roadhouse.

Frost covered every inch of Max's parka, his big mustache, and the whole load on his big sled. He pushed his parka hood back and put his bare hand on his mustache to thaw it out.

"Couldn't be better," he shouted back. He picked some pieces of ice from his mustache. "Nice and hard, no moose tracks."

Charlie Sickik took Max's dogs one by one to the

dog barn. They were big dogs, covered with frost, but still lively. They were happy to be at the road-house again, knowing they'd be warm and fed. Bo and Evalina petted them and hugged their big heads. They loved Max's dogs, and Max's dogs loved them.

But Charlie didn't take Silver to the dog barn. Silver was Max's lead dog, and Silver went where Max went and slept by his side.

Oxadak, Oscar's father, and Dinuk, Jonas's father, started to unload the sled. They carried the big mailbags into the roadhouse while Max and Silver went inside. Max peeled off his clothes and hung them up on the lines over the woodstove. They'd have to be dry in the morning when he took off again, back down the trail. Nothing, Jack and Arvid had taught Bo, was worse than wet clothes in the winter.

Milo gave Max a cup of coffee while everyone gathered around the table to hear all the news. Max took a sip of the coffee and spit it back into the cup.

"I always forget what god-awful coffee you make, Milo," he said. But he drank it anyway after he got used to it.

Max took Evalina on his lap and said, "Well, Bo, where's your partner in crime today?"

"He goes to school now," said Bo. This was the first time she was glad she wasn't in school, because she got to be there when Max came.

Jack pushed open the big roadhouse door, and a cloud of cold bellowed in with him. Everyone shouted noisy greetings at him, teased him because he hadn't taken the time to tie the laces on his big boots. It was like a party when the mail came, Bo thought.

Jack hung up his heavy coat on one of the hooks by the stove and sat at the table. Bo wrapped herself around his huge back and said in his ear, "Do you think my stuff is in the mailbag?"

"Be surprised if it was," said Jack. "Don't get your hopes up."

But Bo was sure she'd have a package. Jack had ordered clay and crayons and paint for Bo from a store in Fairbanks a long time ago. Now her crayons were all broken and the paints in their little cups were mostly used up, and she'd never had any clay to begin with.

Milo set a plate of stew in front of Max. Max fished out a big piece of meat from the stew and held it out for Silver, who took it very daintily with his sharp teeth. Silver was one spoiled dog, all the old-timers said.

Max tossed the keys for the mailbag padlocks to Oxadak so he could unlock the bags, and then Milo dumped the biggest mailbag on the floor.

"Hey!" yelled Max with his mouth full. "Take it easy with that! Didn't bring it four hundred miles through hell and high water for you to bust things!"

Milo started sorting the mail, kneeling on the floor. Jack helped him because a lot of the mail would be for the mine. They made little piles all over the floor. The biggest piles were for the mine, Milo, and the school, of course. Jack looked up at Bo and shook his head. No package for her. Bo pinched her lips together and tried not to feel too bad. Then Jack grinned at her and took a package from behind his back.

"Here you go," he said. Bo hugged the package and smiled.

Everyone in Ballard Creek got a new calendar from the Northern Commercial Company—1930. Bo unwrapped the mine's calendar quickly. She wanted to see what this year's picture was.

"Ptarmigan," she said happily. That was Bo's favorite bird.

Nels's sister had a lot of mail, too. She must have a lot of friends, Bo thought. Maybe they were missing her now that she'd gone. But there were no letters for Nels, because his sister was the only one who ever wrote to him, and now she was here and didn't have to. It made Bo happy to think that.

Milo made up a little bundle for the miners out the creeks—letters, calendars, and packages—and tied it with string. Big Jim would take their mail to them with his dog team, because he had to check his traps along the trail anyway.

There were dozens of new magazines with shiny new covers. Tomas Kovish's magazine had a woman and an airplane on the cover.

"Look, Bo," said Clarence. "This is Amelia Earhart. Woman pilot, really famous." Bo looked at Clarence to see if he was joking, but she could tell he wasn't. She never knew women could be pilots.

Miss Sylvia and the children from the school came banging into the roadhouse to collect the school's mail. Miss Sylvia opened the package from the Department of Education. It was a framed picture of Herbert Hoover, their new president. Bo frowned at the picture. She didn't like the way he looked at all.

Cannibal saw her and laughed.

"He doesn't have a nice face," said Bo.

"That's what I think, too," said Cannibal.

When they got back to the cookshack, Bo opened her package. There was a box of clay in ten different colors, two big tins of watercolors with extra brushes, and most wonderful of all—a big, big box of crayons, thirty-two different colors.

Bo almost drove the papas crazy asking them to read the names on each crayon.

CHAPTER TWENTY-TWO

BO IS SICK

CHRISTMAS HAD COME and gone, a wonderful time. Milo had put a lovely little tree in the roadhouse. When they had the Christmas party, the schoolchildren made a circle around it and sang the songs Miss Sylvia had taught them.

The papas had sent the little bird gold nugget to Fairbanks to be made into a ring, and that was Bo's Christmas present. It was a perfect fit. She could hardly take her eyes off it for the next few days.

◆◇◆◇◆

ONE DAY when it was very cold, the kind of cold that turns the sky and the frost on the trees all pink and beautiful, Bo got sick.

Bo had never been sick before, but she was now. A terrible cough tore at her chest.

"It hurts," she said to her papas, who were more miserable than she was, seeing her so sick. A fever made her head funny; it made her think such strange things that the papas looked worried when she told them.

"It's pneumonia," Lilly said. Lilly knew a lot about doctoring. When anyone in Ballard Creek was sick, she would take a hand in getting them well, though she couldn't do bones. That took a lot of strength, so when there was a broken bone to deal with, people would get Olaf or Big Jim to set it.

Bo was so sick and her breath was coming so hard that the papas were scared. It was the worst time to be sick, the worst part of winter.

The nearest doctor was hundreds of miles away at Fort Yukon.

"At least we can wire him," Jack said.

They wired the doctor in Fort Yukon who wired back a lot of questions. He told them to heat a big bucket of water to boiling, then make a little tent with a cloth over her head and let her breathe in the steam. That would help clear her lungs. He said to give her plenty of water to drink and not to worry if she didn't eat.

Lilly and Yovela came to sit with Bo so that Jack and Arvid could do some of their work. They made the steam tents for Bo and tried to spoon a little custard into her.

When the boys came in to eat, they were very quiet, tiptoeing across the floor. They stopped to look in at her through the door to the back room, their faces serious.

The boys talked at the table about sicknesses. Alex said when he was little, they used to dose everything with kerosene.

"For pneumonia, they would have made Bo swallow kerosene." All the boys nodded. They remembered that.

Paddy said, "And onions. Every time I was sick, my grandma would tie an onion around my neck on a string." The boys all nodded again. They all remembered about the onions.

They were quiet then. They knew how bad

pneumonia was. And they knew there was no medicine anywhere to cure it.

While Bo was sick, three Lapps with a small herd of reindeer came through Ballard Creek on their way down to the Yukon. Everyone was astonished by what the Lapps wore: beautiful clothes made of thick wool in brilliant colors, covered with embroidery.

Jack felt terrible that Bo couldn't see their clothes because she loved color so much. And he was sorry about the reindeer. Bo had longed to see reindeer. And he was sorry she couldn't hear their language. Bo loved to hear other people's talk. One night at the roadhouse, they sang Lapp songs. They were beautiful songs, haunting, and they made the boys sad. Bo loved to hear people sing.

She didn't get better. She got worse, and her red face and ragged breath were horrible. She didn't even ask for Bear, who was sitting on the chair by the door.

Nakuchluk brought her akutaq, and Yovela brought her a little shirt and pants she'd run up on her machine for Bear to wear. Clara and Dishoo, Big Jim's wife, brought her some magazines from the roadhouse. The children at school wrote a letter for her with lots of pictures and their names. But Bo didn't know about these things.

BO GOT MUCH WORSE, and then even worse than that. And then she got better.

One by one, the boys came, just to stand in the doorway and say hello.

Siwash George played his harmonica for her, all six songs he knew, and then "Nellie Bly" again because that was Bo's favorite of the six.

They told her funny stories about how it was when they got sick. They told her about the kerosene and the onion cures. They told her about the Lapps—she was very disappointed about the Lapps.

Jack cooked her all the things she liked best— soft things that would go down easily. He held the spoon for her and coaxed.

"Your favorite pudding, Bo. Pineapple pudding, good for you."

The pudding tasted wonderful, but she felt full after a few spoonfuls. She took another bite, because she couldn't believe she was not still hungry, but she held the custard in her mouth for a while before she swallowed. It was almost as if she couldn't remember what she was supposed to do with it.

Jack said, "Never mind. Your appetite will come back. Just eat a little bit is all I ask."

The next day, she sat up in bed and ate by herself. She ate a little more than she'd eaten the day before. And the day after that, she crept out of bed and got her shoe box room with the cut-out dolls.

Her lovely little bird ring hung loose on her finger, and Jack had to wrap some tape around it so it would stay on.

Then she was getting dressed in the morning, and then she was cutting biscuits, and even though her little face was not as round as it used to be, she was Bo again.

"You look older," said Arvid. "No more fat cheeks."

Bo still felt strange, as though she had been away on a long trip and was learning what had happened when she was gone.

"I saw you by my bed, and you were crying," she said to Jack. Jack's gray eyes were huge and solemn.

Finally he said, "We thought you was going to die."

CHAPTER TWENTY-THREE
THE LITTLE BOY

FINALLY THE DOCTOR in Fort Yukon wired
that Bo was ready to do the things she'd done
before she got sick. Maybe not walk too far at first.
But the papas said she certainly couldn't do anything like what she'd done before—no sliding for
one thing, and certainly no trips with Big Annie in
the dogsled.

Bo wanted to go visiting as soon as she was
allowed out of bed. She wanted to see everyone.
It had been so long since she'd been across the
bridge.

First she'd stop at the roadhouse, where there would be some of the old-timers and Milo, and then she'd go to see Clara, even though Oscar and Lena were in school. She'd tell Clara to ask Oscar to come over to visit her after he was finished with his chores. She'd missed Oscar more than anyone.

Then Lilly and Yovela, and then she'd go to Nakuchluk and Unakserak, and Dinuk and Gracie, and just everyone, if she had time before she had to go back to the mining camp for lunch.

As soon as she walked into the roadhouse, she saw a little boy she'd never seen before. He was sitting at the bar, three stools from the end. Bo was so surprised she didn't say hello to Milo or Jimmy the Pirate or Sol or Charlie Sickik.

She walked up to the little boy and looked at him closely. He was a brown boy with pale green eyes. His eyes were exactly the same color as the aspen bark Bo loved. Bo hadn't imagined that eyes could be such a lovely color.

She knew she was staring, being rude, so she blinked twice to stop herself. He had halfway colored hair, not light, not dark. Just brown.

He was dressed in patched overalls that she knew right away were Oscar's from last year. They were way too big for the little boy; the bottoms were turned up almost to his knees. He wore Oscar's shirt, too, the blue plaid worn all thin at the elbows. And he had raggedy moccasins on his feet. The boy looked at her for a minute, alarmed, and then he looked quickly at his feet, which stuck straight out on the stool.

The old-timers and Charlie Sickik were watching Bo and the little boy intently. Milo was watching too, drying the big sausage platter over and over, forgetting to put it down.

"Bo," he said, "this here's our new little friend."

Bo looked a question at Milo, her eyebrows up. She was like Jack and never used words if she didn't need to. Milo understood her as well as Jack and Arvid did and answered the question she hadn't asked.

He shook his head and put his fingers over his lips. "Not now," he said. Bo knew that meant that whatever he had to say, Milo didn't want to say it in front of the boy.

She turned back to the little boy.

"What's your name?"

"We don't know his name," said Milo. "He won't say nothing."

Bo considered this. If the boy had a mother and father, they would have told Milo his name. So Bo could already see that this boy was alone. Maybe his mama had walked away like hers.

Bo set Bear on the bar top and climbed up on the stool next to the boy.

"What's your name?" she said in Eskimo. The green eyes looked despairingly at her. She said it in English again. He looked away from her, at his two straight legs, and said nothing.

"I'm Bo," she said. "And this is Bear. And that man is Milo, and those are Jimmy the Pirate and Sol and Charlie Sickik." The little boy flicked his eyes over to the men Bo was pointing at. He didn't change his expression at all.

"How come his eyes are that color?" Bo asked Milo.

"My guess is that he's Indian from downriver. Don't look Eskimo to me, and no one here knows him. See lots of green eyes down on the Yukon 'cause there used to be Russians there long ago. Hear lots of Russian names, too."

"Milo playing detective," said Jimmy the Pirate.

"Well," said Milo, "stands to reason."

Bo put her arms around the little boy's middle and lifted him down off the stool. She took his hand and walked him to the Victrola. She put on "Barney Google," cranked up the Victrola, then bent down to look in this face. "Do you like this? It's my nearly favorite song." The little boy looked wide-eyed at Bo.

Bo was disappointed. She thought the music would make him feel happy.

"You want to go out and play?"

Milo shook his head. "I want to keep a close eye on him before I let him go out. I'd hate for him to run away. Maybe he'd try to get back to where they found him."

Bo thought a minute.

"Well, could we have the poker chips, Milo?"

Milo smiled and took the box from behind the bar. All the kids in town liked to play with the poker chips. They came up with more things to do with those chips than Milo thought possible. Bo took the chips to where the little boy was still standing by the Victrola and pulled him down to the floor.

She spilled the chips out—red, white, blue—and said, "You make a stack with the red ones, and I'll do the blue ones."

He seemed to understand right away, and they played together for a while. Then she changed the game and put the chips in a line on the floor—red, blue, white, red, blue, white. He saw right away what the pattern was and made the same lines on his side.

Jimmy the Pirate jerked his chin at the little boy. "He ain't stupid, that's for sure," he said under his breath.

Bo didn't go to see Yovela or Lilly or anyone else in Ballard Creek. All the time she had for visiting she spent playing with the boy.

After the chips, she sat him in one of the cane chairs, and she sat in the chair with him, pointing out pictures in the magazines. He didn't know about turning the pages, so Bo thought maybe he'd never seen a magazine before. Or a book. She knew by now that she wasn't going to get the little boy to say anything, but she didn't think she was making him sad or frightened.

"He does all right with you," said Milo. "He's a bit suspicious of me and the boys here. I thought maybe he'd be okay with women, but he was leery of Big Annie and Gracie when I asked them to have a look at him. He let them give him a bath and all, but he's holding himself tight. You can see he's not relaxed."

It was time for Bo to help Jack with lunch.

"I have to go now," she said to the boy. He looked at her face quickly, as if he knew what she said. She said good-bye to Milo and the old-timers, and she and Bear went out the door.

It was a big heavy door made of split spruce logs, and she was proud that she'd grown enough to open it by herself. Just a little while ago, she'd had to get

someone to open it for her or stand outside and holler if she wanted in.

She stopped outside the door and thought about the little boy. Then she pushed open the door and went back in. He was still sitting where she'd left him. She handed him Bear.

"You can keep him till I come back," she said. "Tomorrow."

He took Bear with a quick gesture, looking hard at Bo with his green eyes.

"I'll be back tomorrow," she said.

She ran into the cookshack, her breath coming in gasps. The cookshack smelled like fresh-baked gingersnaps. It was her job to roll the balls for the cookies so that Jack could flatten them with a cup, but she hadn't been there to do it.

"Oh," she said, "you had to do them all by yourself!"

"Don't give it a thought," said Jack.

"But, Papa, there's a little boy at the roadhouse. With no papa or mama or anything. He doesn't talk. His eyes are green. But his eyes are like something that's dead, like a rabbit that's been snared, how their eyes go funny. Where did he come from?"

Jack walked over to her, wiping his hands on his big apron. He looked surprised. "Forgot to tell you about him. Thought he'd be gone by now. Max found him while you was sick. The last shelter cabin on the trail, that's where he was. No fire in the cabin, and he's sitting next to his father on the bunk. His father was dead. Max guessed it was his father, but no one knows for sure."

"Oh," said Bo, horrified.

"He'd been sitting there some time in that cold shack. Max looked through the sled. He could see the father was going to go beaver trapping, had some marten traps too. It's been pretty cold, but the little guy had a big caribou skin to wrap up in. Lucky, or he would have froze."

"No fire," said Bo, thinking how that would have been.

"Max wrapped the boy in his extra parka and brought him to Milo. Then Clarence and Tomas went back to the shelter cabin and buried the man. Hank'll be able to figure out who the dead man is, seeing as he's the marshal. And he can find out where the little boy belongs," Jack said. "Clarence sent him a wire right away."

"He's got on Oscar's old clothes," said Bo.

"Yeah," said Jack. "They said he didn't have nothing with him, no clothes for a kid in the sled— just what he had on, and that was purely black with dirt."

"He can have some of my clothes," said Bo.

"Sure, Bo," said Jack. "Lots you're growing out of. When the boys go over to the roadhouse tonight, they'll take some to him. We'll look through your clothes now and see what you got that's too small."

WHEN SHE WAS ready for bed, Bo suddenly burst into tears.

"What's up?" asked Arvid, looking surprised.

"I miss Bear," she said. Arvid looked around the room.

"Where *is* Bear?" he asked.

"I gave him to that little boy, just for tonight. I wish I didn't."

"Ah, well," said Arvid. "Lots of times we do something nice and then we're sorry for it. Like the time I gave an old panhandler all the money I had, he looked so beat, and then I was sorry because I couldn't buy cakes at the bakery. I wasn't much older than you. I wasn't a *lot* sorry, I just wished I'd saved a nickel out of that money for my cakes."

"What's a panhandler?" said Bo.

"Someone down on his luck, don't got any money, got to ask people on the street for enough to eat."

"That was nice of you," said Bo.

"That was nice of you, too, Bo. Likely that little boy needed Bear more than you do, all that's happened to him. Likely it will make him feel real good, having Bear. And you can get him back tomorrow."

"I know," said Bo, "but I don't think I can sleep without Bear. And maybe Bear is missing me."

"No, sir. Bear is not missing you. He's happy to be helping that little boy. You gave him a job to do, and he's going to do it. He knows you'll be back for him in the morning."

CHAPTER TWENTY-FOUR
RED BEAR

GETTING BEAR BACK wasn't as easy as Bo had thought.

Gracie, Dinuk's wife, had made Bo a good new caribou ball when she was sick. It was stuffed tight with caribou hair and sewn together with tiny stitches that would never come out. Bo thought a caribou ball would be a good thing for a little boy to play with. So in the morning after her chores, she took it to the roadhouse.

The little boy had climbed back up on his bar stool again, but this time he was holding Bear. Bo pulled his hand to get him to climb down off the stool and sit on the floor with her. She showed him how to sit opposite her, the bottoms of their feet together. Then they rolled the ball between them in the cage their legs made. Bo remembered that's how Arvid and Jack used to play ball with her when she was very young.

He liked playing with the ball, Bo could see. But when Bo handed him the ball and took Bear, the little boy's face looked so hurt that Bo couldn't do it.

She left him the ball *and* Bear.

She told Jack at lunchtime about her problem with the little boy.

"You just ask Lilly to make another bear for him," said Jack. "You know Lilly—she'd be tickled pink to help out."

And Lilly was.

"Don't worry, Bo," said Lilly. "I can make one up for him in a few hours. Got some real nice red velvet. That'll make a good bear. Do you think he'd like red velvet?"

Bo was sure he would.

After supper, Bo asked the papas if she could run

to Lilly's to get the new bear. Jack wasn't so sure she should go.

"Moon's out," said Bo.

"Not worried about the dark, just think you should rest. Ever since you been out of bed, seems like you been running your legs off. Doctor said you could do what you used to, but he didn't know what you used to do. Probably faint if he could see you dashing here and there."

"Oh, please, Papa," she begged. "He can have his new bear, and I can have Bear back."

"What if he doesn't want a new bear? What if he wants to keep yours?"

Bo made a terrible twisty face. "It's red velvet," she said.

"Oh, red velvet," said Jack. "That's different."

Arvid and Jack looked at each other in that way they had of talking without words.

Then Arvid shook his head and said, "Go ahead, but walk, don't run, and come right back. Going to get you in bed extra early for a while till you're completely better."

Bo immediately forgot the part about not running.

She ran to Lilly's and collected the bear. It was beautiful. Bo didn't think she'd ever seen a prettier red in her life. She threw Lilly a happy look and dashed out. And then she ran to the roadhouse to take the red bear to the little boy.

Milo had just put him in bed on a cot in the storage room.

"This is for you," said Bo. "Lilly made it."

She touched Bear. "This is my bear, and this is your bear. They'll be friends."

She was feeling desperate. But his fingers relaxed, and he let Bear drop as he reached for the red bear. He stroked the velvet with such pleasure and made a little sound, the first one Bo had heard him make.

Velvet did feel good. For a moment, Bo wished Bear was made with velvet, but then she remembered about feeling jealous and gave Bear a hug. You had to think what you had was good enough.

Bo made Bear shake hands with the red bear.

"How do you do, how do you do?" said Bo.

She pretended that the red bear answered back in a funny voice, "How do you do, how do you do!"

The little boy's eyes were bright and then he smiled a tiny smile.

"I have to go to bed, too," said Bo. "I'll be back tomorrow."

First she ran to Lilly's. She dashed into the room, almost tripping over Cannibal Ivan, who was visiting. Bo put her arms around Lilly and tilted her face up to look at Lilly.

"Lilly, Lilly, he loved his bear, and he just about smiled. Not a real smile, but almost. I wish you could have seen his face. He really liked the red velvet."

Lilly smiled down at Bo. "That makes me happy," she said.

CHAPTER TWENTY-FIVE

THE LITTLE BOY VISITS

BO HAD MISSED Oscar terribly when he went to school, but now she was so busy with the little boy that she didn't feel lonesome at all.

Sometimes they played in the roadhouse, and sometimes Bo would bring her sled and they'd get Evalina and slide down the riverbank. But Bo was sure the little boy would like going visiting the best, like she did.

She showed him how to sweep the snow off his feet before he went in someone's house. There was always a broom outside everyone's door, and it was rude to go inside without sweeping the snow off.

First she took him to see Tomas Kovich. Bo went through his records slowly. She couldn't read the writing on the records, but she knew from the labels what the songs were. She was looking for the Caruso records.

When anyone bought a Victrola, they got free Caruso records from the Victrola company. Caruso was an opera singer who was very popular. But nobody in Ballard Creek liked him except Tomas, so everyone gave him their free Caruso records. Tomas had a lot of them now.

"That's good," Bo said. "In case you break one, you have a bunch more."

Tomas always played some Caruso songs for Bo, and she thought "La Donna É Mobile" was the best one. It sort of jerked along in a happy way, so that you had to wag your head or something to keep time. She didn't know what the words meant because the song was in a different language, but she swung the little boy's hand back and forth in time to the music and sang very loudly. She only knew the first line, and for the rest she said *da da da dadada.*

The little boy smiled and let Bo swing his hand. At the end of the song, Caruso sang a long, long note, and Bo and Tomas sang it too in a silly way, while the little boy smiled at them.

"I think he likes this Caruso song best, like me," Bo told Tomas.

"Well, it's a good one," said Tomas. "I like it best myself."

"What do the words mean?" Bo asked.

Tomas smiled. "Song tells how no good women are," he said.

Next Bo and the little boy went to visit Clarence in the wireless shack. The boy tipped his head back and looked up to the top of the tall telegraph tower, and he hid behind Bo when she showed him the noisy engine that powered the wireless.

When they went inside the shack, Clarence swung around on his revolving chair and greeted them cheerily.

"Making the rounds with your new pal, huh Bo."

Clarence knew Bo would want him to show the little boy how he sent a wire. *Dit da dit, ditdit*

dadadit, went his little machine. It made Bo wild with excitement to see Clarence's fingers flying. It was like magic. He could talk to people hundreds of miles away, and they could talk to him. She tried to explain that to the little boy, but she could see by his face that he didn't understand.

Each letter had a different sound. Clarence showed them the chart with the letters and the way you made the letters on the machine. "See," she told the boy, "a long line is *da*, and a dot is *dit*." She'd learned that from Clarence.

But it was hard to explain things to someone when you didn't know what language to explain it in.

"When I'm grown up, I'm going to be the wireless operator," Bo told the little boy.

"That's what I thought too, when I was your age. Got me a book of Morse, and I practiced and practiced. Wasn't even full grown when I got a job doing Morse for the railroad. Thought I was a big shot!" Clarence said.

Dit da dit, the machine began to talk, and Clarence wrote down the letters fast. His writing looked pretty messy.

"I got to write it over again after I copy it down," Clarence said. "When I write fast, I get sloppy."

He wrote the message again, carefully this time.

"What are all those numbers at the top?" Bo asked.

"That's the code for the Bettles Wireless," he

said. "And these numbers here are for us, the Ballard Creek Wireless. Every message got to have those. It's the rule."

"Who's it for?" asked Bo.

"I'm not supposed to tell you that," said Clarence. "Wireless supposed to be private." Clarence was quiet for a minute. Then he said, "Wire's for Milo— usually is—just a little talk from his friend Gus at Bettles. Nothing important."

"Oh," said Bo. She'd have to ask one of the papas what private meant. It sounded kind of mean.

Then Bo took the little boy to see Unakserak and Nakuchluk, Big Annie's parents. Unakserak and Nakuchluk were the oldest people in town, and they liked the old ways best. So they'd made their house out of sod when they first came down the Kobuk to Ballard Creek because that was how the Eskimos lived in Kotzebue where they were born.

In the winter when their sod *iglu* was covered with snow, it looked like a hump of snow with smoke

puffing out of the top. In the summer, it looked almost like a beaver dam. In fact the word for beaver dam in Eskimo was the same as the word for house—*iglu.*

The *iglu* was very cozy inside. It had a dirt floor, which Bo thought was a good idea. No scrubbing.

Bo wanted especially to show Unakserak and Nakuchluk to the little boy because they were so interesting. And because there was always something good to eat at their house.

Unakserak was making gravy. That was everyone's favorite thing. The Eskimos didn't use their flour for baking; they used it to make gravy.

"Flour was so special, my father used to lock it up in a box," Unakserak said. "Carried the key with him all times, so us kids couldn't get into it." Unakserak laughed his wild laugh, thinking about that.

Little grease, little flour, water, that's gravy," he told the boy. "You ever eat this?" The little boy didn't show that he had, but he ate a big bowlful when Nakuchluk put it in front of him. Bo felt proud of how much the little boy could eat.

Nakuchluk had three blue stripes on her chin, the tattoos all the old Eskimo

women had. And Unakserak had holes cut in the corners of his mouth for labrets. Labrets were plugs made of ivory, which were fitted into the holes when it was time to dress up.

None of the younger Eskimo men had labrets anymore. Unakserak never wore his labrets, so one of the holes had closed over with skin. The other was still open, and when he ate soup, it leaked, which Bo thought was very interesting.

"Will you show him your labrets?" Bo asked. Unakserak took a beautifully carved little wooden box from a shelf and opened it to show the little boy. His father had carved the ivory labrets from a walrus tusk when Unakserak first had his holes cut.

They had a beautiful swirled design on top. Unakserak touched the swirls gently.

"This is picture of the wind," he said.

FOUR DAYS LATER, Milo got a wire from Hank. He sent Clarence over to the cookshack with it. "Milo thought you'd like to hear the latest," Clarence said.

Arvid raised his eyebrows, surprised.

Jack knew what he was thinking. "Probably

wants to let us know what's going on because of Bo. Her being the little boy's best friend and all."

"Oh," Arvid said. "Sure."

Clarence handed the wire to Jack and sat down at the table. Clarence was happy to come to the cookshack, because Jack always had something good for dessert.

Jack unfolded the wire Clarence had brought. He read it to himself and then he read it out loud to the boys.

Everyone's gone trapping now, so I can't find anyone who knows about the father or the little boy. Might have come from further downriver, Kaltag maybe. I've sent out a wire to every wireless station, so we'll know something soon, when everyone comes back to the village before the snow gets rotten.

Jack folded the wire and handed it back to Clarence.

"Wouldn't think it would be so hard to find out who someone was, would you?" Arvid said.

CHAPTER TWENTY-SIX

THE WIRE

BO AND OSCAR and Lena took the little boy to
Big Jim's house to visit one night after supper.
The women were all sitting on the floor, legs
stretched out, sewing, smoking their pipes. Bo loved
the way the smoke curled around, dancing, and the
way the smoke ran away, scared, when someone
opened the door.

The men were telling stories.

Big Jim especially liked to tell stories about the
dooneraks. Those were little devils or mean spirits
who were all around. Sometimes the dooneraks

helped the anagok, the medicine man, but mostly they weren't helpful at all.

Bo and the other children would get so scared listening to the doonerak stories they had to hug each other all the way home, and Bo would beg Lena or one of the other big girls to go across the bridge with her.

The boy hung on tight to Bo's left hand, and he held on to Oscar's right hand, but his eyes were shining when he watched Big Jim. Big Jim acted out all the parts, made himself big and brave, or shrank down to show how afraid he was. The little boy smiled sometimes when Big Jim did something sudden—threw his arms up in the air or jumped to his feet. Bo watched the little boy and whispered to Oscar, "He's not as scaredy-cat as I am," and Oscar laughed.

There were other long, not-so-scary Eskimo stories about ravens and other animals that turned into people, too, and Bo liked those stories better.

The old-time Eskimos were supposed to memo-rize those stories, every single word, every single gesture. Gracie, Jonas's mama, had told Bo and Oscar how it was done.

"They'd practice over and over," she told them, "say it night after night, same way they raise their voice same place, same way they show with their hands the things in the story. Then their mother or someone would tell them that it was finally right. And then they could say they had that story, that story was theirs, it belonged to them. Then they would start to learn another."

Clara could tell the old stories, but she didn't tell them the same way; she hadn't memorized them.

"I don't have this story," she'd say apologetically. "I have to tell it badly."

That night at Big Jim's, Clara told the story about the man who was mean to his dogs. He had to come back to life as a dog and be owned by a mean person.

"Sometimes, if someone is mean to animals," Clara said, "when he dies, he goes to the dog village, and all the dogs can bite him and hit him with sticks like he did to them."

Bo wished it were true.

MILO TOLD ARVID that the little boy was eating a lot. Arvid said he could see that his cheeks were fatter, his eyes not so sunken in.

"Now that he's had hotcakes, he's a syrup addict. I don't think he ever ate anything but meat and fish before," said Milo.

Arvid made the boy a pair of overalls so he didn't have to wear Bo and Oscar's hand-me-downs. The little boy patted the front bib and looked down at his legs. He was very proud of those overalls.

The little boy was getting used to everyone. When he was pleased, he smiled a big smile now, his eyes round and shining.

But Bo never heard him laugh until one night when Cannibal Ivan was a little drunk and tipped his chair back too far and fell to the floor.

The little boy's laugh crashed out, and everyone in the roadhouse started to laugh too—because Cannibal looked so funny and because it was so nice to see the little boy so gleeful.

He didn't exactly take up laughing in a big way, but sometimes Bo could get him to screetch with delight if she spun him around really fast on the bar stools or if she pretended something silly with Bear and the red velvet bear.

Milo got another message from Hank.

People I'm talking to think the father was a deaf man who was from a camp halfway between Nulato and Kaltag. Called him a wild man because he wanted to stay in the woods. Didn't get along with his own people. Had a wife, but she died when the baby was born. It was a boy, they knew. I'll wire when I've found some relatives.

Milo and Jack talked that over. "Might be the kid just speaks Indian, no English," Milo said.

"Yeah, or if his father was deaf, might be the kid never learned to talk. Think that's possible?"

Milo shrugged. "Well, we know he's not deaf, anyway."

ONE NIGHT Bo brought the little boy to the cookshack to eat dinner. He ate a big supper of roast sheep and mashed potatoes sitting at the cookshack table between Lester and Paddy, who both admired the amount of food he could put away.

After the boys had gone off to the bunkhouse and Bo and Jack had cleared the dishes away, Bo gave the little boy some paper and a pencil and set him to work at the end of the table. He loved to try to draw, but he didn't have any idea in this world how to hold a pencil.

They could hear someone outside sweeping the snow off his feet, and then Milo came in, his face red from the cold. Milo went right to the stove to warm up. He held his hands over the stove, turning them to both sides. Then he pulled a paper from his pocket.

"Wire from Hank." Bo could tell from Milo's face that this time Hank had some news for them.

Arvid took the paper and read it out loud to them.

Found an aunt who lives in Kaltag. She says the boy's name is Grafton. She thinks he was born at Allakaket. She says she can't take the boy, too many of her own, but to send him to the orphanage at Nulato or Holy Cross.

Bo and the papas looked at each other.

"Well, at last," said Arvid.

Bo went to the table and took the boy's hand.

"Your name is Grafton," she said.

He looked at her, shocked.

"Looks like he recognized that," Jack said.

The little boy went back to his drawing. "Say Grafton," she begged him. But he wouldn't say it. He just kept drawing.

"Grafton," said Milo. "That's the name of a doctor was at Allakaket. Must be twenty Indian kids named Grafton after him. Maybe those church women at Allakaket got some kind of record on this boy.

"Well, no way to get him to Nulato now," said

Milo. "I'll wire Hank, tell him that he's got to tell the aunt we won't be able to send him to Nulato till the river's open, another month at least," said Milo, and he left.

There was a silence in the cookshack while they all looked across the room at the little boy. Grafton. He had the pencil clutched in his fist, not holding it the right way at all.

Bo glared at the papas and whispered fiercely, "You said the nun looked mean."

Jack looked unhappily at her. "That was a long time ago," he said.

Bo folded her mouth into a line, the way Jack did when he was thinking hard or feeling unhappy. "We need to keep him," Bo said.

"Now, Bo," said Jack, and Arvid growled at her, the growl that meant not to be foolish.

Arvid and Jack looked at Grafton. "Got to teach him how to hold a pencil," said Jack in a grumpy way. Then they both looked at Bo, both scowling. Grafton didn't look up, just kept fisting his pencil around.

Bo looked at the papas, her eyes wide. It was her begging look.

The papas looked at each other under their eyebrows and were quiet a long time.

Finally Arvid groaned. "Great god almighty."

Jack's mouth was twisted sideways, which meant his mind was troubled. At last he said, "If this don't beat all."

He and Arvid looked at each other, pulling their worst faces.

Bo waited, looking first at Arvid, then at Jack. It was taking a long time.

"Should have seen this coming," said Arvid. He groaned again.

"Hell," Arvid said. He got up heavily, as if he weighed a thousand pounds. He put his palms on the table and leaned forward to look sideways at Jack, asking a question with his eyes.

Jack made a lot of faces, each one worse than the last. Finally he rubbed his head fiercely and said, "Well, what the hell."

Bo stood up so fast she knocked a chair over.

Jack grabbed her by the arm. "Don't you say a word," he said. "Don't you say nothing to him. Don't want to talk about something that ain't going to happen. Don't say nothing to nobody." He scowled at her so severely she bobbed her head up and down fast, to show him she agreed.

"We'll tell Hank to ask the aunt if we can keep him," Jack said, very slowly and carefully. Likely she'll say no. She don't know us, never saw us in her life."

"And we'll tell Clarence not to tell nobody nothing. That Clarence talks too much," Arvid said crossly.

Bo looked so radiant that both of the papas frowned down at her.

"It ain't going to happen, Bo," said Arvid. "No use getting your hopes up. It ain't going to happen, and that's the truth. All we're going to do here is try. No harm in trying. And you don't say a word, not a word, or the deal is off. You hear? No deal if you talk."

Bo shook her head so hard she felt dizzy.

She would not say a word.

CHAPTER TWENTY-SEVEN

MORE WAITING

BO THOUGHT SHE HAD a hard time waiting for things—the airplane, Christmas, Gus's Cat— but there was never such a hard time as waiting for Grafton's aunt to tell Hank if they could keep him.

The days went slowly, slowly. The snow began to sag, the river ice looked tired, and the days grew longer and longer. But still no news. Grafton's aunt was still at the trapline, wouldn't be back for a while, Hank wired.

Everyone in town knew what Jack and Arvid

were trying to do. Bo swore she'd never told anyone, never, and Clarence said he was not the one who told. But everyone knew.

"Stands to reason," said Milo when Jack asked him how he knew. "The way you two are, the way Bo took to the boy. Stands to reason."

When Bo brought Grafton to the cookshack, Jack and Arvid got very busy doing this and that, trying not to pay any attention to the two children.

"Don't want to get too attached to him," Arvid told the boys. "Going to be bad when we have to send him away."

"Too late for Bo," Peter said. "She's got her heart set on him."

Too late for everyone. Now that Grafton wasn't afraid of anyone, he was full of curiosity. He climbed up next to Lester at the cookshack table and stroked Lester's shiny copper hair. The look on Grafton's face made the boys laugh.

"Guess he's never seen such a wild hair color," said Paddy.

Grafton took hold of Philipe's hand with the two missing fingers and examined the empty place sorrowfully. He looked up into Philipe's face as if he were asking how it happened. He examined them all in the kindest manner. He had such a sweet way about him the boys couldn't help but get attached to him.

He took Jack's huge hand and turned it over, palm up and back again. Jack's palm was light, and the top of his hand was chocolate brown. Grafton looked at his own little palm and the top of his hand, and then ran his hand along the line on the side of Jack's hand that divided the colors. He seemed very pleased with Jack's hand.

Grafton talked now, too. Not long sentences or anything, just short words, mostly in English, sometimes in Eskimo. Whatever words seemed right at the time.

He wrapped his arms around Arvid's big leg and looked up into his face. "Big," he said.

"Yes," he'd say when Bo asked him if he wanted to play outside, or "Hurry up" or "*Niaq!*"—stop that!

When Milo asked him what he wanted for breakfast, he'd always say, "Hotcake." Except once, after he'd been visiting Unakserak and Nakuchluk, he said to Milo, "Gravy," instead of hotcakes. Bo thought Milo would never stop laughing about that.

He didn't talk much, but everyone liked to listen to his funny growly little voice.

"Couldn't be said to be a chatterbox," Sol said.

"I think he understands everything, though," said Milo. "If I tell him to do something, he does it, so it stands to reason he understands English."

After a while Grafton took to repeating words. When Cannibal Ivan read a magazine with him, Cannibal would point to a picture and tell Grafton the name. Grafton would say the word, and when Cannibal showed him the picture the next day, Grafton remembered the word.

"Got a good memory," Cannibal said.

Everyone in Ballard Creek taught him words, and he learned fast.

One day Bo pointed to her bear. "Bear," she said. To herself. "Bo." To Milo. "Milo." Then she pointed her finger right in the middle of his chest and waited. He looked at Bo steadily and growled, "Grafton." Milo and Bo cheered.

She pointed to the red bear. "What's his name?"

"Conkers," said Grafton.

"Oh!" said Bo. She didn't know what to think about that. "Milo, what does Conkers mean?"

Milo pulled his mouth down in an I-don't-know way and shrugged his shoulders. "Never heard of it," he said.

Grafton smiled a tiny smile at Milo and Bo, looking pleased at all the carrying on. "Conkers," he said.

He learned everyone's name after that.

BO AND EVALINA and Grafton were playing in the sawdust pit under the saw frame. Sawdust was a good thing to play in at this time of year because it was warm. It soaked up the thin spring sunshine.

Bo'd just covered Evalina with sawdust when she saw Clarence coming from the wireless shack and heading across the bridge to the cookshack. Bo's heart felt strange, as if it were being squeezed. She grabbed Grafton's hand, and they ran after Clarence.

The boys were just sitting down to lunch when Clarence got there. Bo and Grafton were right behind him. Everyone stared at Clarence, who was keeping his face very still.

"Wire from Hank," he said in a strange voice.

Jack searched Clarence's face, and then he took the wire from Clarence and read it.

Marshal at Kaltag talked to the aunt soon as they came back from trapping. I told him to tell her that you were two of the finest fellows who ever lived and you already took in one orphan and are raising her fine. And you'd send her a present.

The marshall wired back—

Jack stopped and looked at Bo and then he read,

She said yes, and when will her present come.

Bo burst into tears and hugged Grafton, who tried to push her away. "Crazy!" he said.

The boys whooped and thumped each other on the back while Bo whirled around the kitchen in a frenzied dance. Grafton began to look scared. Sandor stood up and put his hands over his heart.

"Grafton, welcome to the family," he said.

Jack and Arvid smiled at each other. They shook hands. Jack picked Grafton up and held him high over his head, smiling his biggest smile. Grafton struggled indignantly, so Jack put him down.

"Got us a boy," Arvid said.

"We do," said Jack, and they shook hands some more.

Jack told Bo to sit down with Grafton and eat lunch.

"We'll explain it all to him when you've finished. Right now he looks as if we were all gone out of our heads."

Everyone was smiling so hard they could hardly eat. At last lunch was finished and the boys went back to work, but not until they'd all shaken hands with Jack and Arvid and had hugged Bo and Grafton.

Arvid told Bo, "Don't say anything now. Let us break it to him easy."

"I'll get that old cot out from the storage shed," said Jack. He slammed out the back door and came back with the cot, a thick quilt, and a pillow.

He put the cot right next to Bo's bed and then he patted the cot and called Grafton to him.

"You'll sleep here," he said. He tucked Grafton's red bear under the quilt with his head on the pillow. "He'll sleep here, too," Jack said.

Grafton was looking wide-eyed, like he did when he didn't understand.

Arvid pulled up a chair by Grafton and sat with his elbows resting on his big thighs.

"Well, here's the thing," said Arvid. He looked worried, studying Grafton's face.

"See, Bo says she really needs a brother. That's you. And me and Jack, we really need a boy— that's you, too. So do you think you'd like to live with us here at the mine?"

Grafton's eyes stretched round.

Bo couldn't stand being quiet anymore. "Jack will be your papa, and Arvid will be your papa, and I will be your sister!"

"And you will be our son," said Arvid.

Grafton smiled his secret smile and looked at his stocking feet.

"Do you think he understands?" Jack asked in a worried way.

"He only smiles like that when he's happy," said Bo.

And that was how Bo got a brother. Not in the usual way, but a good way, just the same.

THERE WAS, of course, a big party at the roadhouse to celebrate, and Jack made a big cake with a picture of Conkers in red frosting on the top, which pleased Grafton very much.

Bo spent a lot of time thinking backwards.

"What if Max hadn't been early on his mail run that day? Grafton might have frozen! What if he had been frozen and the doctor had to cut off some toes or fingers? And what if his auntie didn't have too many kids already? And what if it hadn't been winter and Milo sent him off right away and we didn't get to know him—"

"Stop, Bo!" said Arvid. "You're making me dizzy."

CHAPTER TWENTY-EIGHT
NOTHING LASTS FOREVER

ONE SUMMER MORNING just after the cleanup, Gitnoo suddenly turned from doing the dishes, bent to hug Bo, and kissed her. Gitnoo's black eyes were brimming with tears.

"I miss you when you're gone," Gitnoo said in Eskimo, and the tears slid down her face.

"Gone?" said Bo.

Then Gitnoo picked Grafton right up straight off his feet and kissed his cheeks.

"We can't stand it, you go."

Jack looked alarmed.

"What's she saying?" Jack asked.

"She said we're going away, me and Grafton."

Jack looked down at his shoes and shook his head. "I should have known how it would be. Seems like everyone in Ballard Creek knows everything before it's even *happened*.

Gitnoo was sobbing into the dishpan now, so Jack hugged her and then he bent down to Bo.

"We didn't want to tell you till we knew what we were doing for sure." He tilted her chin with his forefinger. "The boss told us last night he's closing the mine. We have to go work somewhere else. Not enough gold this year either. Done run out of ground."

Bo pushed his hand away and glowered up at him.

"I don't want to go," she said.

"I don't want to go neither, Bo. Never felt so bad in my life. But we all got to have a job, and there's no jobs here anymore."

Grafton pressed up against Jack's big leg.

Bo took Graf's hand. "We can't go. He just got used to everyone," Bo pleaded.

Jack sat down and took Bo on one knee, Grafton on the other.

"It's about to break my heart, too," he said.

And that was how Bo and Grafton learned they were going to have to leave their home at Ballard Creek. And that nothing lasts forever.

FOR A WEEK, everyone at the mine was busy making plans. They had Clarence send dozens of wires here and there, looking for work. When Bo asked, "Where will we go?" Arvid and Jack would shake their heads. Didn't know yet.

But in a few days, Clarence brought a wire to the cookshack. After Arvid read it, he pointed to a place on the map. "This is where we're going. Across the Yukon here. Iditarod country. Got a big mining operation there. Lots of mines. We'll be at a mine right here on Innoko Creek, and Lester and Paddy are going to work at another mine a few miles from us. So you'll see them every time they come to town."

"Oh," said Bo with a sudden rush of gladness. Lester and Paddy would be nearby.

"It's not so *very* far away," Bo said. She leaned against Arvid's belly and looked hard at the map. Grafton looked too, clutching Conkers, his eyes wide and sad.

"Well," Arvid said slowly, "it don't look far on the map, but it's a long boat trip. Nearly a month. Fast going down the Koyukuk and the Yukon, but when we cut across to the flats, we'll be against the current all the way. That takes time."

Bo suddenly looked up at him. "But where will everyone *else* go?"

"They got it all worked out," Jack said. "Sandor and Alex are going to be partners and work a claim out on the creeks, near Olaf."

"Oh," said Bo happily. "Near Olaf."

"The boss is going Outside, says he's finished with mining. Peter says he's staying here, going to be one of the old-timers. Figures he's too old to go anywhere else. Then Karl's partnering up with Nels Niemi."

Bo smiled. "They can talk Finn together all the time, then."

Arvid thought a minute. "Guillaume and Philipe and Dan, Siwash George, Fritz, and Andy are going to Fairbanks. Still plenty work in Fairbanks."

"Who will Gitnoo work for?" asked Bo. Arvid shook his head. He didn't know.

NOW THE MINING CAMP was always full of people from town. They helped the boys close down the camp, box up the tools, and cover the shaft carefully so no one could fall down it.

Sandor and Alex and Karl took what they needed for their new lives on the creeks, and Olaf took the extra window glass from the blacksmith shop for his cabin. Big Jim and Charlie Sickik and Dinuk and all the other men took home everything else that wasn't needed—old shovels and rope and all the old lumber. They took the woodstoves from the bunkhouse and the kitchen and all the stovepipe.

The women came and took home the food that Jack had hoarded—dried milk and oatmeal, rice, flour, and sugar—and dozens of useful things from Jack's kitchen. They sent the children across the bridge in a steady stream with bags and wheelbarrows and carts full of groceries and dishes and pans.

The scow took away the boiler and the big bucket from the shaft, the huge kitchen stove, and all the tools and cable and rubber hose that the boss had sold to other mines.

Nothing from the Ballard Creek Mine went to waste.

Bo and Graf spent every minute they could with Oscar and Evalina.

"You remember this when you're gone," Oscar kept telling them. They must remember the saw pit and the spring and the magazines in the roadhouse, Oscar said. They must remember the little frogs who lived in the grass lake by the river. They must remember everything.

"I'll never forget anything, Oscar," Bo told him.

"Unakserak told me *he* don't remember when he was a little boy," said Oscar. "I think you might forget us."

"No, Oscar," said Bo. "I never will ever forget."

THERE WAS a going-away party that lasted all night, with speeches and speeches and more speeches. They talked about everything that ever happened since the mine had opened. "Remember when . . . ," they'd start, and soon everyone would be laughing.

All the women pestered the boys to dance. "Last time I dance with you," Dishoo would say and cry a little.

Everyone who was leaving got a present. Yovela and Lilly made waterproof canvas pants and jackets for Bo and Graf. "For the river," Lilly said.

Nels's sister, Asa, brought new sweaters she'd knitted for them, and Clara brought summer moccasins, big ones that were not meant for this summer, but to fit them next summer. Olaf brought Bo one of Shine's feathers to remember him by.

Every present made Bo cry.

After the party, the boys moved on, one by one. And in a short while, Bo and Graf and the papas were on their way, too.

They left Ballard Creek early one morning before everyone was awake.

"Just can't stand to say good-bye," said Jack. "I think it would surely kill me if everyone came to see us off."

Budu and Big Jim had built them a sturdy poling boat, and Jack and Arvid loaded it with all the things they had to take with them. They had each moved on so many times before they knew just what to take and how to wrap it all in oilcloth and tarps to keep it safe from the river.

There was one thing that was different, though. The boys had given them their Victrola. When it wasn't raining, it sat near the bow on a box Jack made, steadied with rope braces in case they hit some rough water.

The music they played reminded Bo of the people they'd left behind, and all the good times—the dancing in Milo's roadhouse, Lena playing "Bye-Bye, Blackbird," over and over, Tomas playing his Caruso records for them.

"Papa, every song makes a picture jump into my head. Gitnoo and Oscar and the boys and Milo and everyone. It makes my throat hurt."

Jack pulled Bo against his knee and covered her little hand with his big one.

"Look here, Bo. It's not like they dropped off the Earth or something. They'll be our friends forever. You'll write letters just like you wrote to Johnny, and everyone will write back and tell you all the things been going on."

"Johnny never wrote back to me," Bo said.

"Well, he *did*, you just never got the letter yet. You know how the mail is."

Bo began to think about what she'd put in her letters, how excited Oscar would be when he got her letter, and how excited she'd be when she got letters from Oscar, and from everyone—Yovela and Lilly, the old-timers and Olaf and all the others.

Arvid was poling the boat, watching ahead for snags. He suddenly turned and beamed at Bo. "How about someday we'll get in one of them airplanes and surprise them? Fourth of July, maybe, when everyone's there, not scattered all over."

Bo squeezed her hands together. "Yes," she said. "Yes, on the Fourth would be good," she said, imagining how it would be, what it would be like to fly in one of those planes.

After she'd thought about that for a while, she looked in the box under the bow for Milo's favorite record. After she put it carefully on the turntable, Graf wound up the Victrola, and they sat hunched on the toolbox with their knees under their chins singing away, "Yes, We Have No Bananas," the silly way Milo used to sing it.

Down the long, winding Koyukuk and down the silty Yukon, down the Innoko and the Iditarod, Bo and Graf and the papas played their music.

All the way to their new home.

GO FISH

KIRKPATRICK HILL

What was it like growing up in Alaska?
I think I'm beyond lucky to have had all this as a kid—fascinating people, wonderful wilderness, and such freedom. No one paid the slightest attention to us kids, I don't think. We roamed wild and unrestrained all those years, fell in the river a couple of times, broke through the river ice. We rode our bikes for miles and miles on all the dirt roads.

What did you want to be when you grew up?
1. A bush pilot. 2. A switchboard operator for those old-time telephones you've seen in the movies. They were *so* cool, plugging in all those wires at top speed.

When did you realize you wanted to be a writer?
I can't say I ever did until I got seriously broke and was casting about for a way to earn enough money for a new generator. (That's how we made electricity in the bush.) I wrote my first book when I was forty.

What's your favorite childhood memory?
Playing pretend in the old cabins and sheds on our street. Best of all, on a vacant lot was an abandoned stagecoach

used on the run from Fairbanks to Valdez in the early 1900s. Pretend got so *real* when we were little. The things we pretended are sharper in my memory than actual events!

As a young person, who did you look up to most?
Eva Kozloski, my eighth-grade teacher, a unique woman. She was so obviously intelligent, and also funny and quick with retorts—and unflappable. She told us about Einstein and relativity. Since the science curriculum those days was largely about health, you can imagine how that theory blew us away.

What was your favorite thing about school?
Singing. All the teachers could plunk away on a battered old upright, and we had yellow songbooks twenty or thirty years old. We rocked.

Did you play sports as a kid?
Nah. We played baseball in the streets. That was about it. Got my nose broken when someone tossed a bat over his shoulder on his way to first base.

What was your first job, and what was your "worst" job?
When I was eleven, some teenage parents with their first baby left him with me. He was a week old and they were gone all day, desperate to go to a Fourth of July thing. I knew nothing about babies, and I was beyond terrified all day. First job *and* worst job.

What book is on your nightstand now?
Arthur C. Clarke, whom I have never read and thought I should; *Lapham's Quarterly; Don't You Have Time to Think?* by Richard P. Feynman; and I'm reading my granddaughter *The Wee Free Men* by Terry Pratchett. Brilliant. There are a dozen more of

various kinds, including fiction, of course, but I love history and science writing in particular.

How did you celebrate publishing your first book?
Didn't. I was in Galena, on the Yukon, so when I got the letter, the kids and I looked at each other with disbelief for a while, and that was it.

Where do you write your books?
Wherever the computer is.

What sparked your imagination for *Bo at Ballard Creek*?
No imagination required. I'd always wanted to write about the mining camp I lived in when I was little, and about all the other aspects of mining that were around me all my life. I've collected a million stories from the old-timers over the years, and they had to be used.

What type of research did you have to do for this book?
I read a lot of books about Alaska in the '20s and before. I wanted to make sure I got the 20s right because it was fifteen years or so before my time—I was born in 1938. So many of the people I might have asked had died, except for Harold Tilleson and Alan James, who are listed in my acknowledgments. And right after the book came out, both of them died as well. I was so lucky to have them critique everything technical.

What challenges do you face in the writing process, and how do you overcome them?
Sitting. I hate to sit. But the really worst part of writing is the cyclic nature. On Monday, you're pleased with yourself, thinking

the stuff you've just done is quite good. On Tuesday, you read it over and it's "What was I *thinking*!!" Despair settles over you. The next day, you tentatively decide you were a bit hard on yourself . . . it's not all bad. Thursday, it's *marvelous* and you walk on air. Friday, gloom again. It's up and down like that, writing. How do I overcome it? Hmm. I just expect it now, I guess.

Which of your characters is most like you?
None of them, really, though maybe Sister in *Toughboy and Sister* is a bit like I was.

What makes you laugh out loud?
Anything silly. I *love* silly.

What do you do on a rainy day?
I feel absolutely euphoric. I love rain. Also snow.

If you could live in any fictional world, what would it be?
I've lived in a lot of fictional worlds! I lived in Oz when I was a kid; I read every single Oz book. I read once that Gore Vidal lived in Oz, too. First time I knew there were other kids like me.

When I'm writing, I get so deep in the world I'm writing it's a shock to raise my eyes from the screen and look outdoors. It's like having a TARDIS! When I was writing *Bo* and the sequel, *Bo at Iditarod Creek*, I pushed the '20s music tab on Pandora and surrounded myself with Eddie Cantor and all those funny old '20s songs. And ordered old movies from Netflix. It's easy now to be a writer with modern technology, especially Google. My first book was done on an old typewriter in a cabin with no electricity and only a cassette recorder for background music.

Of all my books, though, I think I'd most like to live in Bo's world. My world in the mining camp was something like that when I was a kid, but I've romanticized it, of course, took out all the bad stuff. A world without bad stuff would definitely be one I'd like to live in.

What's your favorite song?
I am obsessed with music, and to name a favorite anything would be impossible. I have thirty Pandora stations and 12,000 songs of my own on iTunes. I will say that I think "Hallelujah" is one of the most beautiful songs ever written (Leonard Cohen), and that Boccherini's "Night Music of the Streets of Madrid" is what I give to all my friends.

What was your favorite book when you were a kid? Do you have a favorite book now?
I loved *The Boxcar Children* so much. Used to play it endlessly, setting up little "camps," with waterfalls to bathe in and so forth. That was my first beloved book, but there were thousands after that. I wanted my first book, *Toughboy and Sister*, to be magic like that.

I often think that I should make a shrine to Andrew Carnegie. What would any of our lives be like without the unquestioned access to a library? What if you could never find answers to all the questions you have? (I'm unhappily aware that I'm talking about the condition right now of most of the people in the world.) Of course, the Internet is even a step beyond that. But for a lot of us, it was the libraries that opened the world.

Who is your favorite fictional character?
Well, every July I read the entire twenty books of the Aubrey–Maturin series by Patrick O'Brian, so you can see those characters have staying power.

What's your favorite TV show or movie?

I love movies. When I was a kid, I fell in love with John Wayne's Irish movie, *The Quiet Man*. I named two of my kids from that movie, and my daughter and I went where it was filmed some years ago—on pilgrimage! Well, that was back then, and this is now. I just saw an indie film called *Junebug* the other day that was beautiful. I don't watch TV, but I do watch Netflix and buy lots of DVDs. I've been crazy about *Firefly*, *M*A*S*H*, lots of cop shows, *Dr. Who*, *Monty Python*. . . . I could go on forever.

If you were stranded on a desert island, who would you want for company?

I have grandchildren and their friends who are more than fun and amazingly clever, and I have children who are the same. I don't suppose it would do to mention Vincent D'Onofrio.

What's the best advice you have ever received about writing?

Never received a shred. That's because I've never known another writer until just recently, and I never talked about writing to anyone except my daughter and my friend Lou. Writing was just something I did on the side to make a little money.

What advice do you wish someone had given you when you were younger?

To make observation one's habit and hobby. I am probably the most unobservant person in the universe. I've walked around in a fog all my life. (A dear friend of ours was missing several fingers and had a glass eye. I never noticed.) I can hardly recognize my own family's various cars, and I was always sure that if one of my kids were missing, I'd never be able to describe their clothes.

Do you ever get writer's block?
Don't think I have. But there have been times when I just couldn't get something right. I've concluded that I need to write with something joyful in the back of my mind.

What do you want readers to remember about your books?
I want people to remember the history, the events, the things that happened in the past, the feeling of those old days. I hate it that people know so little about their own history. I hate it that whole epochs are lost.

What would you do if you ever stopped writing?
Wouldn't miss a beat. I have a thousand interests and things to do, and writing is not one of the most important. After I finish writing about the mining years in Alaska, I'll probably consider my job as preserver of the past well finished.

What do you wish you could do better?
Everything I know how to do I taught myself, therefore I don't do anything well. It's downright embarrassing to be so second-rate at everything.

GOFISH

LEUYEN PHAM

What did you want to be when you grew up?
When I was really young, I wanted to be an actress. Then I turned five and decided that was not the life for me. And then I thought, maybe Princess Leia. Or a teacher. They were both pretty cool to me.

When did you realize you wanted to be an illustrator?
Much later, when I was already in college. I was going to UCLA, studying political science, when I took an art class. The head of the art department at UCLA told me I was in the wrong school and sent me to Art Center College of Design in Pasadena. I never looked back.

What's your most embarrassing childhood memory?
Wearing a KISS heavy metal mask for Halloween one year, because my dad thought it was a witch's mask.

What's your favorite childhood memory?
Playing pretend games with my younger brother. Also, eating summer mangoes!

As a young person, who did you look up to most?
Always and first, my older sister. She was the one I wanted to be like. Next, my teacher, whichever year it was. I loved my teachers.

What was your first job, and what was your "worst" job?
I worked at a fast-food restaurant for a year when I was fifteen. I'd have to say that qualified for my worst job, too—the boys would have bun fights, and always *always* something would land in the chili. Blecch!

How did you celebrate publishing your first book?
I went home and cried, I was so happy. I think that was all I did!

Where do you work on your illustrations?
I have a little studio space where all the magic happens. It used to be a huge studio space, but then we had kids and I had to give up the room. Now, it's a lovely little corner office overlooking the street, with just enough space for a drawing table, shelves, and a computer table. And me, in a rolling chair in the middle.

Where do you find inspiration for your illustrations?
Absolutely everywhere. Memories of childhood, looking out the window, and now—with two little boys underfoot—my kids. I see every aspect of my life in every one of my illustrations. You can't help but draw what you know.

Have you ever been to Alaska?
No, and I've always wanted to go! I think Pat (the author) was worried about that when I first got assigned to illustrate her

book. She sent me loads of photo references and books. But she needn't worry; I'm a pretty devoted researcher. Normally, a trip to Alaska would have been a requirement for me, but the year I illustrated the book we were living in France, and I wasn't able to make the trip. But I will!

Where do you go for peace and quiet?
I live in a house with two little boys, so I don't go anywhere for peace and quiet! I've learned to work in the midst of chaos.

What makes you laugh out loud?
My little boys. And, it's horrible to admit this, but fart jokes too.

What's your favorite song?
"Moon River," as sung by Audrey Hepburn.

Who is your favorite fictional character?
Scout Finch, from *To Kill a Mockingbird*. Love love love that character, and that book. A close second is Turtle Wexler from *The Westing Game*.

What are you most afraid of?
The dark.

What's your favorite TV show or movie?
Oh man! Way too many to list. *Mad Men*, *Game of Thrones*, *30 Rock*, *Star Wars*. Just too *too* many.

If you were stranded on a desert island, who would you want for company?
Dead or alive? If dead, I'd love to hang out with Mark Twain. I have a feeling that guy would keep me in stitches. Alive? Well, my family, of course!

If you could travel in time, where would you go?
I wouldn't go forward. That would be too depressing. And if I've learned anything from the *Back to the Future* movies, it's that you don't mess with time in the future. I would probably travel back to the Belle Époque, in Paris. I would just love to hang with Toulouse-Lautrec, Degas, all those guys.

What's the best advice you have ever received about illustrating?
Don't think! The more you think, the weaker your image will be.

What do you want readers to remember about your books?
I don't want them to remember anything, but I want them to walk away with a warm and happy sensation that lasts the whole of their day, and whenever they think of the book again, they get that same feeling.

What would you do if you ever stopped illustrating?
I can't even think about it! But I'd give writing a bigger go.

What do you like best about yourself?
I am an unfailing optimist and an unrelenting realist, in equal measure. I think I make very good choices because of that.

What do you consider to be your greatest accomplishment?
I don't like to think of any one thing being greater or more significant than another. It somehow feels disloyal to other accomplishments to single one out as the greatest. I tend to focus on what's in front of me and don't bother too much with what I've already done.

What would your readers be most surprised to learn about you?
I can touch my tongue to my chin. I can imitate Betty Boop, but just a little. I once threw a water balloon at the house of a boy I had a crush on when I was ten.

What was your favorite thing about school?
EVERYTHING! I really loved school. My family wasn't very wealthy growing up, and life at home could be difficult. School was an escape, a place I could really thrive at. I always bonded with my teachers, and they in turn introduced me to books that would become my favorites.

What was your least favorite thing about school?
Honestly? Lunch. When I was young, my brothers and sister and I received free government lunches, but they were always awful. String beans that tasted mealy, strange unidentifiable meats, things like that. I was never a big eater, but I remember the lunch lady would never let me leave the table until most of my food was gone. I found ways to hide the overcooked vegetables in my milk carton, and to squish sandwiches down flat enough to seem like I'd eaten most of it.

If you could travel anywhere in the world, where would you go and what would you do?
I would LOVE to go to Antarctica. Just to see the penguins.

Who is your favorite artist?
I don't have one, I have many. Edmund Dulac, Hilary Knight, Tadahiro Uesugi, Alice and Martin Provensen, M. Sasek, the list goes on and on.

What is your favorite medium to work in?
I work in many *many* mediums. I love watercolor, inks, croquille, gouache. Just about anything out there. And digital—it's becoming a favorite too.

What was your favorite book or comic/graphic novel when you were a kid? What's your current favorite?
When I was a kid, *Calvin and Hobbes*. As an adult, same thing. Although *Persepolis* by Marjane Satrapi is edging in.

What were your hobbies as a kid? What are your hobbies now, aside from illustrating?
This is sad to admit, but as a kid, my only real hobby was drawing and writing. I don't suppose I've changed much! Nowadays, I like to travel a lot. And go on hikes with my kids, Adrien and Leo. They're young, only three and six, so the hikes are easy, but still lots of fun.

What challenges do you face in the artistic process, and how do you overcome them?
Every moment of being an artist is a challenge. From conjuring the image to executing it to perfecting it later, each level is difficult and makes me work hard. I tend to change my style with each book, so I find myself constantly seeking out new and interesting ways of creating images. I'm not sure that I ever really overcome challenges, but I'm still trying!

Ever since Bo can remember, she and her papas have lived in the little town of Ballard Creek. Now the family must leave to work far away in Iditarod country.

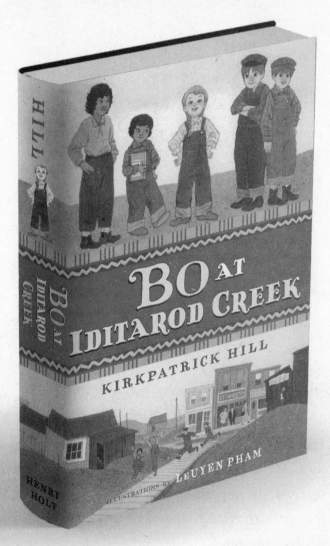

Keep reading for a sneak peek of Bo's new adventures!

CHAPTER ONE

THE PAPAS

Bo's papas were Jack Jackson and Arvid Ivorsen. She didn't have a mama.

Bo started out with a mama, of course. Everyone does.

Hers was Mean Milly—not a nice motherly sort of person, as anyone could tell from her name—but Mean Milly didn't want the job of mama, so she took off. Just before she got on the steamboat headed up river, she marched over to Arvid, who was standing on the riverbank smoking a cigarette, and shoved her baby at him.

A few minutes later Jack came out of the mine cookshack and there was Arvid looking startled, standing on the banks of the Yukon with a baby in his arms, watching the boat go away.

Jack could see that Arvid didn't know one thing about newborns because of the way the baby's head was wobbling around. But Jack was an expert on the subject, so naturally they partnered up to take care of Bo.

And that's how Bo came to have no mama and two papas.

SHE WASN'T long out of diapers when she came to see that it wasn't the usual arrangement. And she could see that hers weren't the usual sort of fathers. People meeting them for the first time would get this look on their faces the way people do when they come up against something out of the ordinary. Trying not to look surprised, trying to pretend they'd seen fathers like that *lots* of times.

For one thing her papas were so much the same. Both massive, with bulging arm muscles straining the sleeves of their shirts. And very tall. You don't often see *one* man that big, and so two of them together is the kind of thing you can't quite take in for a minute.

Other than that they were completely different. Arvid had ice blue eyes and straight Swedish hair, getting a little thin on top. He always swore in Swedish.

Jack was black with smoky gray eyes and a soft Southern way of talking. He hardly ever swore.

Bo called them both Papa, which might have gotten confusing, but it didn't.

When Graf came along, the papas hardly blinked. Just added him to the mix.

Explaining about unusual things can get long and complicated, so when someone asked how he and Arvid came to have two kids, Jack would just smile and say it was downright uncanny how he and Arvid were always both there, right on the spot, whenever someone was giving kids away.

ARVID AND JACK had known each other a long time when they got Bo. Arvid came north during the big Klondike gold rush in 1897, and Jack came a few years later along with hordes of other men. That gold rush fizzled out fast, and most of those stampeders, disgusted and broke, couldn't leave fast enough. But some, like Jack and Arvid, stayed–because they liked the mining life and because they liked the country.

Over the next twenty years Jack and Arvid often crossed paths in one mining camp or another, had a game of cards or teamed up to do some blacksmithing. They were both working at the Rampart mine when Bo happened to them.

Right after that Jack and Arvid went to work at the Ballard Creek Mine up the Koyukuk River. Jack was the camp cook, and Arvid did the blacksmithing. But after they got Graf, the mine ran out of gold, closed down, and the papas had to find another job. They had to leave the place that had been Bo's home for all of her life.

So they were on the way to their new job in a mining camp, which was far away in the Iditarod country. Down two big rivers and up two.

Down was easier because they could just glide along the cold river, using the long pole to steer. Up was harder because they had to travel against the current. Then they might have to use the little three-horse gas engine—but not any more than they had to because gas was hard to come by.

Bo and Graf were under the bow, snuggled into

the billow of down sleeping bags their papas kept stored there. They crawled under there when it was raining or the wind was blowing.

Bo was trying to teach Graf how to think backwards. Graf had only belonged to them for a little while, so she wanted him to see how lucky it was that they'd all ended up together.

But thinking backwards took imagination, and she wasn't sure Graf had any.

It was Jack who had taught Bo how to think backwards.

"A lot of little things have to happen first before a big thing can happen. Really tiny things—things no one would pay any attention to—could change someone's life forever," he said.

Like if Arvid hadn't stopped to have a cigarette, Bo wouldn't ever have belonged to the papas. Just a little, little thing like that had turned her life in a completely different direction.

Bo did a lot of thinking backwards. Jack said she was really good at it, because it was like anything else. If you practice a lot, you improve. But you could get carried away—go backwards on and on, all the way to the beginning of the earth.

You had to know when to stop.

The papas had pulled their yellow slickers on when it started to rain. Jack was hunkered near the bow, reading the water under the brim of his rain hat. Arvid was standing spread-legged for balance, steering the boat with the long pole.

If a wind whipped up and turned the river rough, or if the rain fell so hard they couldn't see anymore, the papas would pull the boat up on the beach, and they'd wait it out.

But it wasn't that bad yet.

It was noisy under the bow, the little waves slap-slapping against the bottom of the boat, the rain-drops drumming over their heads on the wood of the bow, so Bo had to talk loudly.

"See, Max always brought the mail in the winter with his dog team and Silver was his lead dog. But Silver got a hurt foot, and Max had to put him in the sled. And he hooked up Frosty to take his place. But Frosty wasn't as hard-pulling a dog as Silver, so Max was late with the mail."

She paused dramatically. "See, if Max wasn't late, he wouldn't have been behind you and your dad. He would have been *ahead* of you. So he never would have found you in the mail shack. And you would have frozen. And it's all because of Silver's hurt foot!"

Bo thought she had told all this very well, but Graf just gave her a troubled look and didn't say anything.

Bo decided to give up on thinking backwards.

"Do you remember your dad?"

He didn't answer, and she hadn't expected him to. Graf wasn't a big talker.

His dad had died in that mail shack, but Graf never talked about anything that happened to him before they got him. Arvid said maybe he didn't remember, and Jack said maybe he didn't *want* to.

She lay back down and pulled a sleeping bag up over her. The thrumming rain always made her sleepy.

Suddenly Graf's head popped out of the sleeping bag, a tuft of hair standing straight up.

"He got sick."

Bo nodded, startled.

Bo smiled. Graf had started to open up.